Necessary Madness

Necessary Madness

Jenn Crowell

G.P. PUTNAM'S SONS

NEW YORK

G. P. PUTNAM'S SONS
Publishers Since 1838
200 Madison Avenue
New York, NY 10016

Library of Congress Cataloging-in-Publication Data

Crowell, Jenn, 1978–
Necessary madness / by Jenn Crowell.
p.   cm.
ISBN 0-399-14252-5
I. Title.
PS3553.R5928N43   1997   96-38458 CIP
813'.54—dc20

Printed in the United States of America
1   3   5   7   9   10   8   6   4   2

This book is printed on acid-free paper. ∞

Book design by Marysarah Quinn

Acknowledgments

Thanks first and foremost to Madison Smartt Bell for his avuncular advice and tremendous generosity; to Jane Gelfman and Liza Dawson for their sensitivity and support; to Carolyn Mays and Carole Blake for the Pimm's and the marvelous hospitality in London; to all those at the Pennsylvania Governor's School for the Arts, especially Deb Burnham, Melissa Bender, and Corinna Burns, for helping me hit fictive blood and bone; to Susan Dziengeleski, Nancy Springer, and countless others for their encouragement and endless critiques of those early first chapters; and of course to S. Jane Beck-Dettinger, Barry and Bryant Dettinger, Robert, Braden, and Kathy Crowell, Heather Cornell, and the rest of my friends and family for their continuing trust and love.

No-one ever told me
that grief felt so like
fear.

—C.S Lewis

In struggling against
anguish one never
produces serenity;
the struggle against
anguish only produces
new forms of anguish.

—Simone Weil

Chapter One

My husband, Bill, was buried nine years to the day that my father died. During his funeral, I tried not to think about that fact or about the direction my life would now take. I simply stood on the raw ground of the Lamberhurst cemetery with my arm around my son, Curran, and my gaze on the young, shocked faces of the pallbearers as they lowered the coffin into the earth.

Across from us, Bill's mother dabbed her eyes with a tissue and made hysterical, gasping sounds. I drew Curran closer and pressed my cheek to his blond hair. Normally he would have squirmed away, but he stood still until the vicar slammed the Bible closed, as if he sensed the desolation in me.

We all filed back to our cars in somber silence. The January morning was gray and damp, and as I looked over the hill at the old farmhouse where Bill had spent his childhood and at the stark outlines of the bare trees which surrounded it, I thought of the gorgeous weekends when, still innocent with happiness, we'd drive there from London to see Bill's parents. On an afternoon swollen with spring, Bill had painted me running across their lawn and down the slope, my long, dark hair streaming behind me, my sundress billowy, an expression of both euphoria and terror on my face as I flew towards the headstones.

Now, beside my car, I fumbled for my keys.

"Gloria."

I looked up. It was Jim, Bill's best friend from university. I'd never seen him in a suit before, except at my wedding. A huge pain rose in my chest when I saw how perfectly pressed his shirt was. It had been a standing joke that Jim wouldn't recognize an iron if he got burnt by one. There were tears in his eyes.

"Bill was the best of us," he said. "A real purist."

"Yes."

His shoulders shook. "I thought I had things figured," he said. "But now—I mean . . . Christ . . . *Bill.* He didn't deserve . . ."

His words dissolved as his face contorted with sobs. Its soft, pink vulnerability turned some long-rusted key within me, and I embraced him. "I know," I said. "I know." For one dangerous moment, palms against Jim's shoulder blades, I thought of my father.

"Mum." Curran's small, plaintive voice. "Gran needs to talk to you."

We pulled apart. Still distraught, Jim walked away, raising his hand in farewell just as my mother-in-law put hers on my arm. "Please come up for lunch," she said, voice pleading yet cautious, as if she expected me to lunge at her, given the slightest provocation. "That is, if you want company."

I didn't, but her pale hazel eyes were so forlorn and the house over the hill held so many reminders of Bill that I nodded. "I'd like that."

A light rain drummed on the windowpane as I sat on the living room's plaid sofa with a quilt draped over my shoulders, my legs tucked under me, and my fingers wrapped around a cup of Earl Grey. Bill's father stoked the fire while his mother cleared the plates of roast beef and mango chutney from the table. I ran my tongue over my lips, remembering the gentle, sleepy hours of early evening when their son and I had lain beneath blankets, reaching our hands under the sheets to memorize each other as we listened to water pound on the roof and promised ourselves just ten more minutes before we'd get up to raise the drawn shades and start supper.

"Would you like some more tea, dear?" Bill's mother asked.

"Yes," I said. "Thanks, Louise."

She came in from the dining room and handed me a second

cup, gazing at me with a mournful look on her face. She stroked back a lock of my hair. "My favorite daughter-in-law," she said, a joke since I was her only one. Her eyes were red.

When we had first met, I had found her nervous, mousy, almost subservient in her eagerness to please, but I'd liked her despite her quirks. After twenty-one years with my mother the fashion goddess, I was delighted to meet a woman who answered the door wearing jeans with holes in them.

Now she sat beside me on the edge of a corduroy wing chair. "Gloria," she said, "I want you to know that you're always welcome here. You'll bring Curran to see us, won't you?"

"Of course." I glanced around. "Where'd he wander off to?"

She laughed. It was the tremorous, broken laugh which had tumbled from my mouth countless times, the pained peal of a mother fighting to keep herself under control. "The darling. He volunteered to do the washing-up, can you believe?"

"Just like his father," I said. I took a sip of the tea, then set it on the table. "When I met Bill, my friends told me I'd hit the jackpot. An artist who could actually balance a checkbook and cook and clean."

By the fireplace Bill's father wiped the moist corner of his eye with his thumb. He caught me watching him, and I smiled; he turned his head. I felt as if all day I had witnessed and validated the grief of others—Jim, Louise—while my own lay submerged, waiting to spring out, not in acceptable expressions of tears or eulogies, but in a frantic plea, an angry shout, fingernails scraped down an innocent cheek.

We heard a banging noise from the kitchen.

Bill's mother stood. "I'd best go check on him," she said.

I watched the tail of the old workshirt she'd changed into flapping as she retreated. My eyes grew heavy. I spread the quilt over myself, curled up on the sofa, and stared at the wildflower pattern on the tea saucer before me until I drifted off to sleep. Drowsiness had always been my escape from pain. After my father, after the bullet, I'd slept for two days.

When I awoke I heard Curran and Louise talking in the kitchen. Bill's father still sat by the fire. I hugged my knees and watched the flames and played a maudlin game of could-have-been, wondering if Bill, had his white cells not staged a coup, might have been like him at sixty. Would he have smoked a pipe and wrapped himself in green wool cardigans? Certainly he'd have been gentler than his father; he'd readily admitted that he was easier on Curran than his father had been on him. Even when he had every right to, Bill never raised his voice at our son. He had the amazing ability to convey firm, deep disapproval— whether it be over Curran's grade on an exam he forgot to study for or the way I treated my mother—with a few simple, quiet words, an arm placed knowingly across a shoulder. I would have snapped at Curran over anything—a door slammed, clothes left scattered on the floor—had it not been for Bill. *Don't,* he'd say, as his wide-knuckled fingers worked out the brutal knots of tension in my neck. *It isn't worth it. Relax.*

Bill's father cleared his throat now.

"There . . . there are some old sketchbooks in the attic," he said. "Things of Bill's. You might have a look. Curran's interested in art, isn't he? Perhaps he'd like to see them."

I rose and stood beside him in my now-wrinkled black dress and stockings. I'd always been a little afraid of him, what with that gruff voice and pretentious name: *Edward Ladbrooke Burgess*. When I'd come here to dinner for the first time, he'd shaken my hand warmly, but his face registered pure disapproval of the fact that the girl his son had chosen to marry was not a gracious English flower, but a reticent American exchange student going through a punk phase. I didn't forgive him for his snap judgment, but now I longed to rest my hand on his shoulder and soften him with human touch.

"I'll go ask him," I said.

We climbed creaky stairs in the darkness, ascending towards the gabled attic. "Are there bats?" Curran asked.

"I don't think so," I said, "but if it'll make you feel better I'll go first and check."

I gazed into the main space. Behind me Curran swayed without a rail to grasp and reached for me to maintain his balance, his hand against the small of my back. I thought of Bill's fingers stroking my spine, awakening my flesh.

"We're fine," I said. "No bats in sight."

I guided him up the last few steps. The dusty stillness of the attic was eerie, as if Bill had just run down to the kitchen for a bite to eat and would soon return to his charcoals and oils and brushes. I stepped around coffee jars and newspapers from the seventies, picked up a sketchbook, and sat on the window ledge to thumb through it. The first pencil drawing I came to was an image of a narrow-faced, dark-haired girl who at first glance looked like me. The caption beneath her read SARAH. Probably one of his first girlfriends, judging by the adolescent penmanship. I frowned and turned the page. The next sketch was a color portrait of Louise, perfectly capturing her complaisant eyes and mop of brown hair. I grinned.

I flipped through a few pretty but dull drawings of ivy-covered trellises, outbuildings, and gardens. Then I leaned back and wiped the grimy window so I could look out of it. From where I sat, I saw the cemetery and its freshest grave.

"Do you remember," I asked, "when we'd come here to visit your grandparents and you'd always ask to go to the cemetery because you were afraid the dead people would get lonely?"

Curran pretended not to hear me. He skimmed his hands across the battered easel, the table draped with canvas, the dried colors encrusted on a palette. Finally he spoke. "No," he said with a sharp, angry incredulity I'd rarely heard before in my mild, docile child. "That's daft." He shrugged. "But I suppose I was little then."

How quickly a child forgets, dismisses with a wave of his hand. Whole years obliterated. I was five; I'm eight now. A sage. Ludicrous.

Would he forget the sound of Bill's voice? Would the scent of his father fade from his memory?

When he'd been younger he'd adored the cemetery. He'd begged me to read him the names of 1800s stillborn babies that were inscribed on the cracked white tombstones, and soon he could rattle off the birth and death dates of all the beloved mothers, daughters, sons. He spoke of the dead as if they were friends with distinct wants and needs and personalities, and picked flowers to adorn their graves. "Let's go see Hannah Cartwright," he'd say, as if she were a lovable old aunt who'd greet him with tea and biscuits and open arms when he arrived. "Can she hear us?" he asked once.

I swallowed. "No, sweetheart," I said. "When you're dead you can't see or hear or do anything."

"Oh," he said, and wrinkled his eyebrows, mulling over the idea for a moment. Then he ran to find a person with a tall headstone whose ledge he could jump off.

Today he'd wandered away while Louise was asking me to lunch. I'd turned and seen him standing by Bill's grave, his head down. He was small in his brand-new black suit. His fair hair blew. The look on his face said: *So this is it.*

Now he fingered a box of pastels. "Gran gave me this big lecture while you were sleeping," he said. "About how I'm the man of the house now, and I'm supposed to look out for you and not mind if you get a bit mental since you're sad."

Please not again, I thought.

"Curran," I said. "Come here."

He turned and came over to me, his expression solemn. I held out my arms. He leaned into them, resting his cheek against my shoulder. He smelled of chalk and peppermint and naiveté shattered.

"Don't worry about me," I whispered onto the top of his head. "Promise me you won't."

Against the wool of my dress he nodded. I clutched him to me and closed my eyes. In my mind I was far from the farmhouse and its rustic charm; I was across the Atlantic Ocean, in the house of my childhood, an ivory palace full of chandeliers and spiral staircases and walls I couldn't brush my hand across and carpets I couldn't walk on in my shoes, and I was hearing a Vivaldi cello solo, my mother's screams, the terrible, mournful sounds of my father's weeping.

Chapter Two

When I'd been twenty-one, I'd boarded a plane to London under the guise of studying English literature in the land where it originated, but I'd really gone for two other, paradoxical reasons: to escape from my parents, and to see firsthand the frighteningly seductive country where my father had been born, and where my mother had fallen in love with him. During the flight, I scrawled a youthful, defiant declaration in my journal. "Even if for some weird, creepy, Santayana-esque reason I end up marrying an Englishman and having his child," I wrote, "I swear to God that I will never, ever become as bitchy and unfulfilled as my mother or as sad and sick as my father."

A month later, I met Bill. He was blissfully normal; I was aching for oblivion. At first I thought I'd have no trouble keeping my promise.

But now, after Bill's death, I sensed the awful aspects of my parents within me, sure as a pulse. The question which for years had lingered in the back of my mind jumped to the forefront of my consciousness: What if I *am* like them?

I needed details. I needed to hold the circumstances of their lives and mine with them, like tissue-wrapped angel statuettes shoved in a box and left untouched for a decade, mouths cracked and noses chipped, ceramic ivory luster soured to a dingy yellow, their folded hands and wide-eyed beautiful stares subversive, wasted figures clasped to the heart then slammed at the wall.

And so I struggled to resurrect them. My mother, Caroline, was the one who set the rules about not walking on the carpet with shoes on or not brushing a hand across the wall. Jaw set, short blond hair brushed severely off her forehead, she swished when she walked. Her strong, square features and mocking, pale-blue eyes endowed her with a haughtiness which made her fascinating but kept her from being called pretty. She was one of those women who insisted on mascara and heels for a Saturday grocery trip, one of those rare chameleons who could be on the verge of a nervous breakdown when the phone rang and still answer it with an even-tempered "Hello."

She gave cello lessons at home, not so much because we needed the money but because she claimed she'd go crazy if she didn't have something "nondomestic" to do. To say she was talented would be understatement; she'd studied at Juilliard and gotten her master's overseas. She pined to join a symphony and travel the world, if only for the theatrics: first-class flights, roses in her hotel room, long, flowing black skirts to wear for performances, the pride of seeing her own intense face bent over the strings in a close-up shot broadcast on public television.

But she couldn't. She had me.

"I grew up in an age when success was a diversion for a year or two before marriage," she told me once when I was older. "You're lucky, Gloria. You can do what you want; there aren't any pretenses. Back then, though, the only reason we strove like hell to get into a good school and earn the diploma was so we could entice men with our intellect. Ha."

She never said outright that I was the tether keeping her from the concert halls of Paris and Vienna, but her resentment rooted itself in every pore, affecting the way she treated both me and her students. More often than not she drove them from the house in tears because of her criticisms, knowing her music had taken on the same numb timbre as theirs.

My father, Riordan, was so gentle by contrast that when I later thought of him I was reminded of the Jains, those men of India who sweep bugs from the sidewalks lest anyone tread on them. He taught chemistry at a nearby community college, and loved to recount tales of kids who almost blew the lab to bits. His dinner conversations were wild tangents on how every atom gets recycled, how nothing ever disappears.

"Just think," he'd say, gesturing widely over the spaghetti, "you—*you*—could have the atoms of Albert Einstein within your body."

My mother would roll her eyes. "Oh, for Christ's sake, Riordan," she'd say. "I can't tell relativity from chickenshit. You know that."

Marvelous though my parents' exchanges were, they had a pattern which puzzled me. My father's earnest intensity met my mother's sarcasm like a hand desperately reaching to touch an averted face. They'd stare at their plates, scrape the last bites of food into their mouths, gulp water. By the time I was six, I'd mastered the art of talking to fill gaps, whether it be about what I wanted for Christmas or someone throwing up during social studies. Soon my mother would push her chair away from the table and announce she had a lesson in a few minutes. Then my father would murmur that his stack of tests wasn't going to correct itself.

While my mother complained if I knocked on her door while she was teaching, my father always left his study door open. I'd lean against the jamb and watch him grade in the green glow of his banker's lamp, one palm flat on the page, the other hand gliding out 72s and 85s and 90s, never in red ink because he was sure it caused students unnecessary anxiety. His face was thin and boyish in the light. Prematurely gray hair wisped in silver half-moons around his temples. "Come on in, love," he'd say, in that marvelous British voice which sent a delicious shiver up my backbone. "Don't be shy."

When he'd finished his work, I'd sit on his lap and draw lopsided hearts and stars and rainbows on his desk blotter while he told me stories about how life was before I was born. Basic facts became myth in that little room; our family timeline blurred to a watercolor mandala amongst the musty textbooks and cordovan leather. Mommy had been the glowing muse, vibrant with the scent of hope and gardenia perfume. She had taken his hands and forced him to live again; she had enveloped him in flames and burnt his pain to ashes as they danced into the morning. I pictured this: their bodies slowly revolving in smoky air, roles reversed, his cheek buried in her neck, her fingers caressing his back. "And you lived happily ever after, right, Daddy?"

"Of course," he said, and his voice never faltered.

His stories were reassurances. They balanced the sharp spaces between my parents' words, their jabs and pointed glances. The picnics, the leisurely walks through narrow streets, the afternoons spent painting their "grotty" first flat in the Australian ghetto of London's Earl's Court, getting less paint on the walls and more on each other—all his nostalgias lulled me into a candy-coated haze which promised me that if happily ever after had been possible then, it was possible still.

In hindsight what shocked me wasn't the fact that I swallowed his sugary morsels of memory. What shocked me was the fact that, twenty-five years later, the truth remained nebulous. Did they really kiss in stairwells and giggle over the fortunes in their cookies at Chinese restaurants? Maybe, but in retrospect the pastel web my father wove felt like a blinder, a narcotic, a wistful man's skirting of actual experience. His recollections were dense whispers at the edge of my ear as I sat on his lap and drew, while we both struggled to convince ourselves that the exuberant angel

he once knew and the elegant, fiery shrew across the hall screaming at little girls for horrible intonation were one and the same.

The only concrete evidence was photographs. They were
taken in clumps like clots of blood, one event to a roll. My parents lying on their stomachs on a beach towel at Eastbourne, his
arm dangled around her shoulder, their grins crooked. She wore
a yellow bikini, and her mouth hung open, slack with laughter.
My father gazed down, his nose sunburnt. A thermos (of lemon-
ade? brandy? no telling what) lay between them. Another picture
showed them caught in a doorway in a pinched embrace on New
Year's Eve, he suited, she in velvet cloak and fur beret, cheek to
cheek. Someone's noisemaker was stuck by his ear.

There were two other snapshots, however, which stuck in my
mind for many years, mainly because of the fact that in both, my
parents wore the same clothes, giving the pictures the Before/
After quality of a ghoulish makeover.

In the first, they sat on a blanket in the grass, beneath a tree.
In the right-hand corner the massive stone of a college building
loomed behind them. They were on their knees, the remnants of
lunch—what looked like the core of a Cox's Pippin apple, the
ubiquitous thermos—spread about them. Once again his arm was
around her shoulder. Her hand grasped his. He held her tightly
against his chest, as if she might fly apart if he let go. Her head
was tilted, and her eyes gleamed. She wore a white peasant
blouse and a skirt dotted with wildflowers, dark blue or black—in
monochrome, it was hard to tell. A girlish mischief I'd never seen
in her shone on her face. My father looked the same as he did
when I knew him, except that his hunter-green jacket with the

leather elbow patches was new and his hair was darker, almost black as mine. His eyes were closed, chin down at an angle, lips poised to skim the side of her thin, smiling mouth. They looked giddy, my sweet, ravenous father and my mother who couldn't tell relativity from chickenshit but had a Fulbright to Oxford. Under closer scrutiny, though, it was obvious they were pulled by different desires, in opposite directions. My father itched to gather her against the rough fabric of his shirt and rasp, "Don't leave me, don't you ever," and while my mother glittered with photogenic playfulness, her body arched, she strained to tumble past him into a space of her own.

In the second photograph, taken a few months later, they were on the QE2, heading back to the States so my mother could hit up her rich relatives for money. They'd stay for decades, first near Philadelphia, in Bryn Mawr, where she'd grown up and would soon give birth to me in the steamy twilight of a summer evening. Later, lured by the modest promise of my father's teaching job, they'd relocate two hours west to another small Pennsylvania town, which my mother would describe as "death by quaintness," charming to the point of suffocation, a far cry from London, cultureless, conservative. There, in a huge brick Colonial house funded by her parents, they'd languish in an upper-class-wannabe neighborhood, slowly sinking down into the too-new elegance, learning to distrust each other. But they didn't know that then.

In both snapshots they wore the same skirt, the same jacket, the same smiles, but a subtle distance lay between them, so subtle the passenger who kindly captured them on film probably couldn't see it. My mother's face was fuller. Her eyes crinkled with an emotion too frustrated for elation, too ladylike for anger. Her hair, still long—she'd cut it off after she had me—was drawn up with barrettes, an impish, childlike touch, but some of it had come loose and whipped freely in the ocean air. She held a straw hat banded by navy grosgrain ribbon. My father held her elbow. There was a vacancy in his squinting gaze, a passive acceptance that they weren't sailing towards, but sailing away. They kept their backs to the deck railing, to the water, to the horizon.

And of course there was another crucial moment, one not suitable for Kodak. After I'd become a mother myself, and had known the perverse, maddening experience of raising a child, I thought of it often. I imagined the famished hour of my conception.

I pictured their bedroom with its cherry suite, its gold baroque mirror, its china baubles and doilies on top of the dresser. I saw him ease back onto the bed's heavy rose-colored comforter, hands laced across his stomach as he waited for the moment when her stubby musician's fingernails would catch wool threads as she lifted his mulberry sweater. She stepped forward, knees against the mattress, and shoved her straight, glistening hair behind her ears. He watched her with a languid smile as she unbuttoned her cornflower-blue silk blouse, then her skirt, revealing the dip of her breasts and her quivery ribs, the empty bowl of her stomach and pinch of navel, the pomegranate cave which was her heart. "Please," he would say, voice pathetic; in my mind she would have red marks on her shoulders and back from where he gripped her so tightly. She'd slide down in an arc like a diver to meet him, bone over bone, because she was young and flattered and not yet a bitch and because she wanted to yield to him, to the swell in her blood like the thrill of a full orchestra.

Did he whisper to her that if she gave him the chance, he would make her life beautiful? Did she have any idea of his warped longing, his pain's magnitude? I thought so. After me, the merry clusters of photographs grew smaller and smaller.

Chapter Three

Those first few weeks after Bill's death, I expected to wake up each morning and find the windows smashed, our bedroom walls gutted, the whole city lost in the senseless echo of grief's reverberation. Instead I found only myself, curled up under a fortress of blankets, shivering, in the middle of the mattress.

When Bill had been in the hospital, I'd risen before my alarm every day, jittery with expectation and false hope, pacing barefoot on the cold floor before I went into the kitchen and gulped countless cups of black coffee while I made French toast for a still-slumbering Curran. Now, however, my drowse-heavy hand reached out by reflex to press the clock's snooze button two or three times as I dove back down into turbid oceans of sleep, awash in dreams of a shoulder to bury my face in, a body to coil around, until I felt small fingers shaking me, a small voice calling into the depths, *Mum, you must wake up*—Curran's fingers, Curran's voice, urgent, scared, sweet.

I could hear him slamming cupboard doors and opening and closing refrigerator drawers in the kitchen as I hurriedly yanked on my nylons and learned to anticipate his shout of "I'm making you breakfast!" while I bent in front of the mirror, still blurry-eyed, to put on my lipstick. I'd come out to find him already dressed for school, hair better-combed than mine, homework and books already in his knapsack on the floor, a plate of buttered toast and a cup of amaretto, with cream and sugar, awaiting me on the table. "Since when did you learn to make coffee?" I asked, yawning.

"Last week. Your lipstick is on crooked."

I swiped at it with the side of my hand.

"Other side. There. It's brilliant now."

He reminded me so much of Bill. I sat down at the table and picked at the toast. "I'm not that hungry," I said. "Here, take some of it."

"No," he said, shaking his head. "I ate already, and besides, you're getting dead skinny, Mum. You should eat more."

I smiled absently. Slumped there, I felt like a passive verb. A child.

"What time is it?" I asked.

"Time to leave," he said. "I called Mrs. Romdourl downstairs. She said I can go to school with Raj."

He slung his knapsack over his shoulder and headed for the door, terribly small yet terribly wise in his navy-blue sweater. A shot of longing tore through me.

"Hold on a minute, love," I said.

He turned. "I need to go. We get demerits if we're late for morning assembly."

Before, I'd always had to scream down the hall at him to get him out the door. *Quit poking around, or you'll be in trouble!* Bill would lope into the kitchen in his old faded robe, just up, and kiss me on the side of the neck, his mouth imprecise with half-sleep. "A few demerits never hurt anyone, love. I had plenty."

Now I held out my arms. "Not enough time for a hug goodbye, at least?"

He ran over, embraced me hard. I closed my eyes, whole again, right again. "You've got a button missing on the back of your dress," he said.

"Don't worry about it," I said. "Go on."

The door banged closed behind him. I felt down my spine, found a spot of unadorned wool, rested my head on the table. I was already twenty minutes late for work. And he was right.

I taught English at a comprehensive school just outside of London. I'd stumbled upon my career guided by echoes and a sense of defiance; I'd seen too much of my mother's artistry wasted to want to emulate her, and chemistry was out of the question once I got old enough to debunk the farfetched magic of my father's theories. English, therefore, had seemed a viable choice for me in college, a sort of middle ground where articulateness and freakishness, finally, wouldn't be branded one and the same. The last thing I wanted was to become a floaty, surreal muse infatuated with language (my father's dream daughter), or a useless pedant bulldozing tight-faced through Bakhtin (my mother's object of contempt), so I'd been elated when I'd gotten the rather pragmatic job offer seven years earlier. I had summers free, got to banish the word *polyglossia* from my vocabulary, and learned incredible patience on the days I wanted to strangle every sullen fourteen-year-old who sat down in my classroom and proclaimed each work we studied "a bunch of bloody rot."

Their lack of decorum aside, most of my students and I got along well. They complained about my tough grading, but loved it when, on dreary winter mornings when none of us were in the mood for Chaucer, I let them lounge on top of their desks and just talk. "Listen, you guys," I'd tease the ones with the nose rings, "I was around for the *real* revolution."

They'd gasp and fight to defend their cherished quasi-individuality. "No, you weren't," they'd say, eyeing my suede heels and Marks and Sparks sweater with such suspicion that the next day I brought in a picture of myself at fifteen. The room rang with their howls of laughter at my rags and dyed hair and black lipstick, but after that, they bitched about their essay scores a lot less and paid attention to my lectures a lot more.

During the long ordeal with Bill, they'd displayed a gritty

compassion of which I'd never thought adolescents were capable. They never commented on the way my hands shook while I handed back papers or the tremble in my voice when I read off that night's list of reading assignments after I'd gotten a call from the hospital. They asked about Bill often, with refreshing bluntness oddly similar to that of my son: "Your husband, has he got better yet?"

"Not yet."

Wicked yet shy smiles. "Well, once he does we're throwing you a party."

"God help us that day," I'd say, broken inside, laughing.

Now, though, once they'd seen me come back a week late from Christmas break, hollow-eyed with exhaustion and ten pounds thinner, once they knew there wouldn't be any wild celebration, they were different. They still made their usual boisterous room-entering noises, and rolled their eyes at announcements of what to them were disgustingly early paper-topic deadlines, but they never joked anymore, never begged for a "telling Chaucer to bugger off" session, as they'd referred to them when they thought I was out of earshot. Instead they concentrated on my lectures with a control so rigid it was eerie, and when they worked together in groups they actually whispered and kept on task as opposed to engaging in loud discussions of who pulled who on the secondary-school circuit the previous weekend.

Had this transformation been under other circumstances, I would have been delighted, but now I saw it as a subtle betrayal of trust, a terrible foray into the twisted world of adult social graces, as if, like Curran in his grandmother's kitchen, they had been advised to tread lightly with me, Mrs. Burgess the mental, the literature instructor gone unhinged. Countless times when I wrote assignments on the blackboard or leaned over to read a student's introductory paragraph, I longed to whirl, to grab their gritty tough-but-innocent shoulders, to cry out in a strangled, intense wail, "I'm me, I'm still the hardnosed grader with the punk stories, still the one who can make you laugh and piss you off when I deduct for spelling, and we can still tell Chaucer to bugger off occasionally, I'm the same, grief hasn't transmuted me, don't you see?"

But sometimes I had trouble believing.

At night, taking the tube home, huddled inside my coat, I bit my fingernails to shreds and watched ubiquitous blond girls in leather jackets hop on and off at stations, their bodies thin as mine but glowing, gliding effortlessly through the dull metal of the sliding doors while mine shivered, spluttered its refrain of cold, winter, loss, there is no escape. The blooming flowers of Northern Line graffiti swam before my eyes, their red-and-blue swirls reminding me of the bouquets in mid-wilt all over my living room, my dining room, my kitchen, and with them the people I had to thank for their kindnesses, their saccharine words, their carnations.

I tipped my head back. The world roared past me in the darkness. In my mind I gave myself instructions in much the same way as did the silky, disembodied voices on the tube platforms who gently chastised all passengers to mind the gap and cheerfully announced that the next station was St. Pancras.

When the signs on the wall slow down enough to be read, when they stare at you, endlessly repeating ANGEL ANGEL ANGEL, that piercing word he was, you'll get up, you'll shove your way out, you'll mind the gap, you'll ride the escalator up to the turnstile in the slick brightness, your eyes will mist but you'll blink, pretend to read the ads for Harvey Nic's, Dillons, the Tate's latest international exhibit, oh Jesus that one will hurt but you'll keep on moving, you'll shove the card in the slot, watch it pop up, no wavering here, and then out into the open, into the murderousness of winter, you'll walk towards Upper Street, you will ignore the rosy-cheeked families of three, four, sometimes five but not often, not usually two, not ever two, you will look past the wool-sweatered husbands and their trench-coated wives who don't deserve them, you will grit your teeth if you have to and turn onto the side street that is yours, make your way up to the walk that is yours, to 10a Theberton, the round green door and frozen empty windowbox, slick streets and streetlamps aglow, it is like you dreamed it when you were twenty, it is like you dreamed it but with a piece cut out, oh Jesus this will hurt but you go up the front steps, you take the stairs two at a time, you are shivering, you want warmth, you want arms and fingers and voices and mouths to surround you, you're crying, you let yourself in, into 10a, you have minded all the gaps and watched for rapidly closing doors which when obstructed, you know, are dangerous, and you are home but you are alone, the flat is a mess, there are too many flowers, too much fecundity in the face of this barren hour

of five o'clock, but you'll wave to your son when he barrels in,
you'll smile through the wet mask of tears that has covered your
face, you'll come inside. And I did.

In the evenings, after I had crouched on the edge of the bed and
cried for what felt like the ten millionth time, after I'd peeled out
of my stockings and dress and yanked off my earrings, I crawled
into the bathroom's old claw-footed tub and soaked in water so
hot it verged on painful.

There in the ragged comfort of walls' peeling paint and the
half-glow of dim lights which shrouded the mirror, my shivers
dissipated as my hair fanned out around me. As the water grew
tepid, I thought briefly of winter afternoons stark with magic
when, young, absorbed, I'd scrubbed the splashes of paint and
turpentine from Bill's neck and shoulders in the same porcelain
tub; he got so involved when he painted, with his whole body
practically, his lack of inhibition both hysterically funny and ad-
mirable to watch. "God, you're a mess," I said. "How do you get
like this?"

He pretended not to hear me. "Something a lot of artists
don't understand," he said, "is the basic concept of ephemerality."

"As a limitation?" I asked, running a hand gently through his
hair. A cascade of green paint flecks rained down. "Most attractive, love."

He grinned. "As a limitation, yeah, but also as progress. Part
of doing anything creative is learning when to trash it. When to

let go. Being able to work on something for five, ten years and then smashing it to bits because it doesn't work, because it's stale now, and then assimilating the dead good aspects . . . that's progress."

Ephemerality. I had to laugh now, thinking about how naively I'd slid closer to him, rested my cheek against his soapy shoulder blades, and thought, *Screw the ephemeral, screw progress. I will never let go of this.*

Eventually I would hear the loud door slam that was Curran coming upstairs from his friend Raj's (he had his own key now, now that I couldn't always be trusted to wake up and get home on time and be a concerned mother), and soon a yell of "I'm making sandwiches; shall we have roast beef or ham?"

"Roast beef!" I'd yell back. "And how many damn times do I have to tell you to come in quietly?"

It wouldn't hit me until I'd grabbed my bathrobe and headed down the hall to change into my jeans that lately I sounded like a frightening fusion of my parents' faults: my father's neediness, my mother's temper. And there would be Curran in the kitchen, still in his school uniform, dutifully spooning chutney. Fragile kiss on the cheek. "Did you have a good day, Mum?"

I should be doing this, I thought, sitting down at the table and for the second time in one day watching him grab napkins, pour tea (he knew how to boil tea *and* make coffee? had Bill taught him that? or was it Louise during her postfuneral lecture?), slice more bread for me. He munched away at his sandwich, one leg kicking his chair—"Stop it," I said. "I don't need a headache"—while I vowed to get up earlier in the mornings, to quit wallowing in tears and torrid water after work so I could be in charge again, if only for him. In Curran I searched for signs of my own quiet, perverse childhood, huge-eyed sorrows and disturbing precocities, but found none. *You see?* I told myself with the false brightness of rationale. The fact that he felt compelled to perform these small, tenderly executed duties, to make me sandwiches and alert me to my crookedly applied lipstick, wasn't what bothered me. What bothered me was the fact that, as with Bill, I had come to expect them.

One night in late January, I lay on my back beneath a red plaid quilt, shivering as I chewed one fingernail until the blood surged in my mouth. Light from a streetlamp outside spilled hieroglyphic shadow-symbols across the bedclothes.

The door opened. My breath grew tight. Every time I saw a hand on a doorknob, my body stuttered with delusional hope. But no. It was only my son. "Mum," he whispered, "it's suppertime. Are you going to get up?"

I nodded and turned on my side, propping on one elbow. He sat beside me on the mattress.

"Shall I ring the take-away man for Chinese?" he asked.

"Sure." I stroked his hair. He didn't squirm or protest my touch, but rather sat still and looked away from me, his face alarming in its stoicism; I knew what he really wanted was to run down the hall and order sweet-and-sour prawns, yet he knew he had to indulge me. I drew my hand back.

While he made the call, I stumbled into the bathroom and

splashed water on my face and tied back my hair. After a decade of living with the idiosyncrasies of British heating, I'd grown used to wearing two pairs of socks and enduring a perpetual slight chilliness, but following Bill's death I'd grown colder. I grabbed my robe from its hook and wrapped it around me.

The doorbell rang. "My wallet's on the hall table, Curran!" I yelled.

After a short pause I heard him call back, "I don't think it's the take-away man, Mum—he hasn't any boxes and he doesn't look very Chinese."

"Well, that's nice and ethnocentric of you," I said as I came into the kitchen. The man at the door, with short, gleaming black hair and disgustingly white teeth, laughed. In his silk shirt, black jeans, and Doc Martens, he looked like just another thirtysomething Islington trendy, a brand of creature even I, the romantic Anglo-American, couldn't hide my disdain towards. The memory-taste of vodka bobbed in my throat when I noticed the combat boots.

"Gloria Burgess?" he asked.

"Yes."

"I'm Jascha Kremsky." He offered his hand. Though I assumed from the name that he was Russian, his accent was hard to place.

"And your point is?"

"I'm a sculptor at a co-op in Chelsea. The . . . the same one Bill belongs to. Belonged."

"Oh. Come in."

His name didn't sound familiar. Then again, there'd been so

many in that group, so many who'd sat around our kitchen table
with jumpy hands and excited voices and quasi-sophisticated
chatter. The ones closer to him—Lorin, Sean, Taylor—had been
at the funeral.

"Sorry I didn't ring first," he said. "I hate to catch you at such
a bad time and interrupt your dinner, but since I was just in the
area I thought I'd stop by."

"You don't have to apologize," I said, motioning towards a
chair as I dropped into one next to it. "Any time is bad around
here lately."

"I'm sure it is." I liked the flatness in his voice, the objectivity
it held. No pity, no mournfulness, just acknowledgment.

"Would you like some tea?"

"No, no thank you. I'm fine." He leaned back in his chair.
"What I've come to talk to you about is Bill's work."

"His work?"

"Yes. Specifically the idea of a retrospective."

"It's not usual for an artist to get a retrospective at the age of
thirty-two, is it?"

"No, but Bill wasn't your run-of-the-mill artist, was he?"

His voice was soft, eulogistic, coaxing.

"Let me ask you something," I said. "Why now? Why not six
months ago, when Bill was euphoric and sure he was going to
survive, when he would have loved to do a show? Why not two
months ago, when he was getting sicker but still creating? Why
not the night before he died, when he was pumped full of morphine, for Christ's sake? Why the hell now?"

Jascha stared straight at me. I admired him for not flinching.

"There were some paintings," he said, "that Bill did in the last few months of his life. I've seen them at the co-op. They're extremely powerful and innovative, they're—"

"Enough criticspeak. I know which ones you're talking about."

"What I'm getting at is that they have a lot of pulling power. Which is not to say that his earlier works are bad pieces, but would they attract large numbers of people? No. However, with the inclusion of his last paintings, especially under the circumstances, since they detail a man coming to terms with his mortality—"

"What you're basically saying is that the only reason my husband is worth a retrospective is because dead people are more interesting." He nodded. "That's the most repulsive, exploitative thing I've ever heard."

The doorbell rang again. Curran, who'd been sitting and listening to our conversation with a mixture of fascination and fright, ran to answer it. This time it was the take-away man.

Jascha watched as Curran handed over a ten-pound note in exchange for a huge box and a plastic container of wonton soup. "How old is your son?" he asked.

"Eight."

His face softened. "He's a cute kid," he said, and then returned to his persuasive speech. "You must understand, Mrs. Burgess, that no one's intention is to exploit Bill. We just have to hit the right time, the right climate."

"Victim art," I said. "Controversy. I understand full well what you're saying, but I still think it's sick."

"I'm sorry if this sounds harsh, but there is a commercial aspect to the promotion of art. One I don't think Bill fully realized or wanted to acknowledge."

Yes. That was Bill—gentle, idealistic, art-will-conquer-all. The last few months, he'd come home from the studio with a daub of green on his cheek, a smudge of sepia across his nose. He'd speak in TV-movie clichés like "I think I'm going to beat this thing." I kissed him and said I was glad. Stupid, stupid darling. Did he really think he could stop leukemic cells with a paintbrush?

"It'll be big," Jascha said. "It'll be very tastefully done. We're hoping to get the Hayward or Whitechapel."

At the counter, Curran struggled to get the lid off the soup. "Watch what you're doing," I said, "or you'll splash it all over yourself."

"Don't you think that is what Bill would have wanted?" Jascha asked.

"I know this is what Bill would have wanted," I said, and stood. "But I also know that any maudlin memorial or trendy display could never pay homage to who Bill was. He was too complex."

"So you aren't giving us permission for the project?"

"You're very bright." I led him to the door. "Now I'd appreciate it if you'd get the hell out so my son and I can eat dinner in peace."

He drew a piece of paper from his pocket and handed it to me. "My number. In case you change your mind."

"I don't intend to."

He stepped outside, then turned around to say more. "Mrs. Burgess—"

I slammed the door on him.

After dinner I sat at the kitchen table and stared at the wadded napkins, the smudged water glasses, Curran's aborted homework, which was so illegible it looked more like the Cyrillic alphabet than a set of multiplication problems. I felt split open. My throat hurt even though I hadn't been yelling at Jascha.

One afternoon years ago, Bill and I had gone museum-trekking in the middle of winter and I'd forgotten my gloves. When we came home he sat me down on the red paisley couch in the living room, knelt before me on the floor, and massaged my numb hands. "This is going to hurt," he said, and it did. They were great stabs, those pains of regained feeling, and I felt them again now.

Curran padded back in, barefoot and fresh from his bath, clad in pale blue flannel, hair damp. A comb swung in his grasp. "Come here," I said. "Let me get the knots out for you."

He came and turned his back towards me so I could get the most unruly bit at the nape of his neck. His warmth comforted me. I ran the comb's teeth through the moist tangled curls, and saw Bill's hair, soft and brown and falling out in clumps.

Curran wriggled.

"Mum," he said, "if there's an exhibit of Dad's, can I go to it with you?"

"There isn't going to be an exhibit."

He whipped around to face me. "But you said that that's what Dad would have wanted."

I set the comb on the table and took his face in my hands. "Forget about it," I said, and kissed his forehead. "Put some slippers on and finish your math, all right?"

That night I had the dream.

I was standing with my father in total darkness at the side of the M6 motorway to Manchester. Suddenly two cars came from opposite directions, washing us in the terrible gleam of their headlights and slamming into each other. We saw the driver of one car, a young girl, fly against the windshield, her eyes wide. "Adrienne," my father sobbed, and clutched me to him, burying my face against his chest and holding me there until I suffocated.

I'd dreamt the same thing for years. This time, though, I didn't startle out of sleep right away, like I normally did. I dreamt that Jascha Kremsky held my head under in the River Lethe, and I fought, unable to decide whether to struggle to the surface or let the water take me down, torn between the need to remember and the desire to forget.

Chapter Four

After a while my father tired of the stories about my mother as muse. Then on our nights in the study, he began the saga of Adrienne.

She'd gone to secondary school with him back in Manchester. She'd sat in front of him in sixth-form English, and during the class he'd stared at the gorgeous dark hair she wore piled on top of her head, all but one seductive wisp, which trailed down the back of her high, classic neck.

He couldn't concentrate on Keats because of her. She was

afraid she wouldn't pass her A-levels in Maths because of one dreadful chapter tripping her up in calculus. He tutored her; she lent him her meticulous notes. By exam time, they were in love.

Like all my father's stories, it was waiflike, sweet, and tinged with cliché, but as a child I loved it. "Tell me more," I begged. "About her pretty-colored sweaters, how she had one for each day of the week. About how she used to amaze the teachers by using such big words in class."

Beautiful though she'd been, Adrienne had, like my father, also been a loner. "She understood perfectly the difference between loneliness and solitude," he said, "and she was brilliant. For her, talking about existentialism and literary theory was ordinary conversation, natural as discussing what to have for dinner."

Although I had no idea what he meant, I nodded happily and leaned my head against his shoulder, transfixed by his language and his tales of such a marvelous creature.

"She was delicate," he said. "Strong of mind, but that very strength gave her delicacy. I had to protect her. I had to watch out for her. She could have been taken advantage of easily."

I couldn't imagine him ever protecting my mother.

"That woman was a gift," he said. "There I was, this tall, skinny lad, friendless, in threadbare sweaters with unkempt hair—and to think that she loved me, that she would be the one . . ."

More than his other stories, these quickly degenerated into mumbled monologues on how undeserving he'd been.

"But you were both different. You were both alike," I said, picturing the two of them, twin geniuses trapped in the gray maze of a northern city, sitting in a cold, drafty classroom and thinking solemn thoughts as they turned their heads from the teacher's too-easy lecture to stare out of windows spattered with rain.

"Yes," he said. "It was the two of us against the world, and we were winning."

One night he showed me a picture of Adrienne. He took the second volume of the encyclopedia down from the shelf and flipped to the page with an article on Robert Browning, where he had placed the photograph. "Her favorite poet," he said. "She said she loved him because he pursued communion with the world to the point of audacity. His friends used to think he was crazy because he ate flowers."

"That *was* crazy," I said.

"No, it wasn't," he said. "He wanted to take in everything."

"Well, they must have tasted awful."

He laughed and handed me the picture. In it, Adrienne smiled, the soft smile of a girl who, like her favorite poet, wanted to take in everything. Her hair curled around her ears and down past her fragile shoulders, and her face was bony and narrow. She wore a pair of dangly glass earrings and a dark sweater whose neck came down in a sharp V. Her eyes shone.

"She looks a lot like me," I said. "I mean, she's much prettier, but . . ."

"Ah, child, you've got my talent for self-deprecation," he said, and drew his arm around me. "You look exactly like her."

I turned the photograph over. On the back Adrienne had written him a message in handwriting so ornate it looked like calligraphy. I struggled to read the words. She'd quoted a stanza of "Two in the Campagna":

Riordan—

> *I would I could adopt your will,*
> *See with your eyes, and set my heart*
> *Beating by yours, and drink my fill*
> *At your soul's springs—your part, my part*
> *In life, for good and ill.*

Although R.B. would probably doubt me if he were here, I have, love, I have, and I shall never go back to seeing any other way.

—Adrienne

Later on, at college, I would analyze that poem, prattle for fifteen pages of explication about spiritual unity and elective affinity and how echoes of the piece's theme could be found in the work of Graham Greene, but at that moment as a nine-year-old all I grasped in the archaic phrasing was the sheer power of love. The dangerous kind of love that happens once and only once, that either heals or scars, melds or shatters.

"Does Mommy know about Adrienne?" I asked.

"She knows she existed, yes," he said. "She doesn't know how much I loved her."

"Did you love her more than Mommy?"

He gazed out the open door. We heard a brisk request from

across the hall. "Could we take it from the second measure, *please!*"

"Adrienne was pure," he said. "Your mother is all veneer. She isn't real."

"So why did you get married?"

"She was a warm body. She was there. She was witty and sharp-tongued and eager, and I needed to forget."

"Forget what?"

He leaned down and kissed the top of my head. "That's another night," he said, "but now it's your bedtime."

He and Adrienne had gone to Oxford together, two of only five from their class to be accepted, their faces shining and oblivious with youth as they stood on the train platform, Adrienne in a soft green floral dress with a cream-colored shawl around her shoulders, my father in his one well-worn suit, waving to their families with relief at the knowledge that they, the gifted ones, wouldn't suffer their parents' proletarian fate, not with degrees in literature and chemistry. Then they dashed onto the train, grabbing each other's hands with giddy excitement as they watched the smokestacks of factories roll past, eventually giving way to the somber lushness of a university town—or so they thought later on, his arms around her, his cheek against the back of her neck as she read passages from Joyce to him, curled up on the window seat of her attic bedroom while in the pubs the rest of Oxford's students laughed their ale-thick way through another pint of bitter.

Their final year there he asked her to marry him. Of course she said yes.

"We were so incredibly happy," he said. "We had the wedding set for July—we wanted the traditional June, but we knew we'd go barmy if we tried to get married during finals—and our whole lives figured out. We were both going to go on to graduate school, and she was going to teach and write—she'd already been published—and I was going to teach as well, and we were going to be academics for a while, a Renaissance couple, and then have children. . . ."

"Why didn't you?"

He sighed and rubbed his temples. "She died," he said.

It had been a Friday night in early December. He and Adrienne had planned to drive home to Manchester to see their parents for the weekend. My father had had to stay late to monitor a lab project, so that night she made the drive home alone.

"We said goodbye out in the quad," he said. "It was snowing a little. She had on a deep-blue scarf and a white beret. She glistened. She kissed me, and her mouth was warm in spite of the cold. 'Don't torment yourself too much with the analysis, Riordan,' she said. I wanted to pick her up and hold her in the folds of my jacket. I wanted to breathe her in. I told her to ring me up as soon as she got home, no matter what the hour, and to be careful. 'When have I ever not been?' she said. And then she ran across the lawn, car keys jangling in her hand, coat billowing."

"What happened next?" I asked.

She'd been about to turn onto the M6 when a car swerved across her path and hit her head-on. She'd flown against the windscreen with a motion so violent it had broken her neck, that high, classic neck at which my father had gazed with such rapture during sixth-form English. The driver of the other car—possibly drunk, but who was to say?—kept right on towards Birmingham on foot and was never found. Adrienne died instantly.

I trembled. While before the study had been cloaked in a soft warmth, it now felt harsh and cold. The glass which covered the top of my father's desk was the glass of the car's windscreen, and the glow from his banker's lamp became the gleam of oncoming headlights, the last thing Adrienne saw.

"Don't talk," I said. "I don't like this story anymore."

"Why do you keep calling it a story?" he asked. It was the first time he'd ever spoken to me roughly. "This is her life, *my* life."

He put his head down on the desk and sobbed. It was a wrenching, pitiful sound; it dug into me and made me want to cry with him and at the same time make him stop. I wrapped my arms around him and pressed my cheek against the back of his neck. "Please don't," I whispered. "Daddy, please don't."

In a few moments he quieted. Slowly he rose up again, his face flushed and mouth contorted with pain. I grabbed some tissues from a box on the shelf behind me, and sat gingerly on his knee. With one hand I steadied his quaking shoulder. With the other I dabbed at his tear-stained cheeks. "Please don't cry," I said. "You're scaring me. Please. That was a long time ago. It's okay now."

In her music room my mother screamed, "You call that vibrato?" while I blotted his face again and again, and still the salt trickled from his reddened eyes.

Chapter Five

A few days after I'd slammed the door in his face, I called Jascha Kremsky. "You're the last person in the universe I expected to hear from," he said.

"I owe you an apology," I said. "You wanted to have a calm discussion, and I behaved like a shrew."

"I'm the one who should be sorry, seeing as I barged into your flat at suppertime and fed you a line of postmodernist crap when all you were expecting was Chinese food."

I laughed.

"I had no right to act as if I knew what your husband would have wanted," he said.

"No. You didn't."

"But I'm still devoted to the idea of the retrospective. Not for the sake of controversy or trendiness, but for Bill."

"How well did you know him?"

"Not very, I have to admit."

"Then why are you so devoted?"

"Every day, Bill came into the studio ready to get down to business," he said. "He never sat around bullshitting about artistic responsibility the way the rest of us did when we were stuck on a piece and didn't know where to go with it. Bill always knew. And he never spoke about his art. Hell, we'd talk and talk about what we were going to do until the energy dissipated and we didn't do it, but not Bill.

"I'd watch him walk in," he said, "and he'd have on an old coat and a plaid shirt and a scarf tied around his head, after he'd lost his hair. Some days he only stayed half an hour, he was that weak, but he came."

Behind me I felt Bill as a phantom lover, his mouth on my neck, hands sliding down my arms, dredging up the goodness within me.

"Mrs. Burgess? Are you still there?"

I jumped.

"Yes," I said, twisting the phone cord around my finger, "and please, call me Gloria."

"Gloria, I'd like you to reconsider."

"Why do I get the feeling that you're not going to give up until I do?"

"Because I won't."

"I don't know. It's just—it's not something I think I can deal with. You've got to understand. Getting up in the morning is hard right now."

"I understand."

"And I don't mean to offend you, but I've seen the kind of affected, marginally sincere stuff your group tends to put on, and I don't want it to be—"

"I'll give you full say in all aspects of the project, final approval of all decisions, but I'll try to make it as small of a burden on you as possible."

I sighed.

"All right," I said.

His voice filled with relief. "Thank you," he said. "You won't be disappointed."

About a week later, he asked me to come into the studio and look over the pieces he'd selected as possibilities, and I agreed to meet him there one night.

It was eerie going back to the place where Bill and I had first met. Sometimes when he worked there in the evenings, I'd meet him at the studio and we'd eat at a chip shop across the street. I'd always felt a little uneasy standing there in my big black coat with my hands stuffed in my pockets, an anomaly, a lone once-academic female in the midst of twenty male artists who scraped and banged and swirled away at marble, wood blocks, and canvas while loud rock music grated. Even when I had an enraptured

Curran with me, I never thought of the studio as anything more than an annoyingly incongruous but vital backdrop to a life my husband loved. Now, however, with him gone, the place was imbued with an almost mystical significance, a wild energy which turned the track lights into radiant beacons and the industrial discord songs into wrenching anthems.

When I arrived, I found Jascha sitting on the window ledge. "You made it," he said.

"Did you think I stood you up?"

"I wouldn't put it past you."

He led me into a small room off the main workspace. Its shelves held a variety of audio-visual equipment. In one corner sat a cart with a television and VCR. On the far wall hung a movie screen.

"What, you didn't make me popcorn?" I asked. I'd forgotten that some of the group members were into film production.

Jascha laughed nervously. "You amaze me," he said.

"Why? Do you think that just because currently my life is hell I've lost all sense of humor? Granted, it was a bad joke . . ."

He pulled a box off one shelf. "We're lucky that we've got slides of all the work he'd done as a member," he said as he set up the projector.

I sat on the faded green couch which smelled of ale and cigarettes and feverish idealistic dreams, and Jascha dimmed the lights and sat beside me. "You realize," I said in the darkness, "that I won't be able to look at this as an art critic like you will."

"Yes."

"I won't be able to judge perspective, or form, or chiaroscuro."

"I know."

He clicked the first image onto the screen. The motion was almost comical, reminiscent of basement vacation showcases, only this time the slides weren't of the Grand Canyon or Hawaii, but my husband's inner landscape.

"I liked this one," he said. "I thought it was youthful, delicate. The color's terrific."

It was the painting of me running down the hill at Bill's parents' farmhouse in Lamberhurst.

"Is that you?" he asked.

"In my younger days."

"Oh, come on," he said. "How old can you be? Twenty-nine? Thirty?"

I nodded. "That wasn't long after we got married. It was the most innocent, ridiculously happy time of my life."

"Ever?"

"Ever. We were drunk on each other. We were oblivious. We were saturated in the kind of joy that makes you think you're invincible, armored, but really leaves you open to attack."

"If you were so happy then, why does your face look so terrified there?"

"I'm not sure," I said. "I guess I've always been ambivalent."

I rubbed my eyes. We'd been looking at slides for two hours, and we'd only advanced three years. I hadn't realized how prolific Bill had been.

"Are you okay?" Jascha asked. He touched my shoulder. I jerked up.

"I'm fine. Really."

"Why don't we take a break?" he said.

We went into the kitchen, and I sat on the table, still in my good silk skirt and heels from work, while Jascha rummaged through the refrigerator.

"I married the last man who was in this kitchen with me," I said.

He glanced over. "What?"

"Don't worry; I was only being reflective. It wasn't a warm-up to a proposal. Although I firmly believe that history repeats itself for those who let it."

He grinned. "Let's see," he said, "we've got half a head of lettuce, a bottle of mineral water, a beer—"

"Grab that. I'll split it with you."

"Seriously?"

"Seriously."

He poured two glasses, handed me one, and sat beside me. "Does this bother you?"

"Would I be doing it if it did?" I took a sip. "Actually, it does. It hurts the way every reminder of him hurts. Living without him, though . . . that's what really bothers me."

I leaned back and laughed.

"I suppose you think this is funny," I said. "Or at least mildly amusing. Here you are, wanting to do something very controlled, very logical, a *project*. And you have to deal with me, the melo-dramatic widow."

"I don't think it's funny," he said. "Though I must admit,

when I went to see you I never expected you to chew me out in your bathrobe."

I stared down into my glass. "It's so strange," I said, "but since Bill's died I feel like I'm becoming the very woman, the very mother, I swore I'd never become. People I talk to—my sweet Indian neighbor who lives below me and watches Curran sometimes, the other teachers in my form—keep telling me how strong I am, how well I'm coping. But I'm not. I'm dangerous. Because grief is essentially selfish. Grief is essentially hunger.

"God, the person I swore I'd never be, the things I swore I'd never do! Every day I'm amazed at the soap-opera actress who's me. I find myself getting maudlin. Of course I'm allowed to, but . . . I find a sweater of his draped across a chair and I cry. I set out three plates instead of two. All that Monday-night-movie shit.

"Bill was my anchor. My friends used to tease me; they said I was emotionally dependent, but I could never explain to them just how Bill made me feel. He was a man who inspired lightness, who made you feel as if whatever badness you had in you was purged. Whatever wrong you'd done or had done to you was forgotten, forgiven."

Jascha watched me with a pensive look, mentally recording every detail while maintaining the kind, probing gaze of a psychoanalyst—*go on, continue, yes, of course, every nuance is relevant, every thought matters.*

I set down my glass. "Well, this isn't helping us to choose paintings, is it?" I said.

"No," he said. "Look, maybe we'd better call it a night. We can finish another time."

I checked my watch. "You're right. I ought to get home to my son."

I slid down from the table and smoothed my skirt.

"You do understand," I said, "that despite what I told you, Bill was not a saint?"

"Yes," he said. "I do."

"So there really is going to be an exhibit, Mum," Curran said as he crawled into bed. "Can I go to it?"

"I don't think so," I said, and sat beside him.

"Why not?"

"Oh, it'll be boring."

"How do you know?"

"I've been to shows before. They're just a bunch of people standing around drinking wine and acting like they're smarter than they are."

"I don't care."

"We'll see," I said. "At the rate the plans are progressing, you'll be twenty before the exhibit opens."

He lay back on the pillows, face soft and perfect with satisfaction. "Then I can go and drink the wine no matter what you say," he said.

I laughed, and held out my arms to him. "I love you," I said, and breathed in his scent of talcum and freshly washed hair that sent splinters into my heart.

"I love you, too," he mumbled. I closed my eyes and felt him quiver in my embrace. He's one-half Bill, I thought; he could *be* Bill, in that twisted logic—the logic of atoms—

"Mum," he said, "please turn out the light."

I let go of him and sat up. Lately I'd sensed in myself a desperation, a clinging desire driving me, and in him an impatience, a sullen silence born of anger. Most of the time I played strong and he played well-behaved, but who knew, who knew?

I reached to switch off the lamp. I glimpsed my hand—a mother's hand, a madwoman's hand—and it scared me. "Sweet dreams," I said. The words tasted like gravel.

Chapter Six

After I heard the story of Adrienne's death, I began to have nightmares about her. I saw her hand fly up in protest, and her eyes widen with terror as her neck snapped like a doll's. Sometimes it would be me in the car, driving towards my death. I'd wake just before the awful metallic sound of the crash, my nightgown drenched with sweat, my breath a pronounced rasp. Still delirious and drowsy, I'd climb out of bed, stumble towards my parents' room, and wrench open the door.

Incredibly enough, it was my mother who crawled from the

sheets and came to me, glimpsing my mute three a.m. anguish. Night softened her. She didn't complain about being awakened, but instead put her strong, bony hands on my shoulders and led me back to my room. "It was only a dream," she said over and over, her voice hypnotic, as I lay on my back on the mattress and gripped her warm fingers and stared at her calm face, thinking, *I am not Adrienne.*

But in the hours of daylight I wondered. What about what my father had said at the dinner table that one night? If my mother could have the atoms of Albert Einstein in her body, couldn't I have those of Adrienne? Wouldn't that answer the question of why my father indulged my mother as if she were an insolent child, and why he saw me as his brilliant adult confidante? Wouldn't it explain why he gazed at me with a look of such sad, pitiable yearning?

Saturday afternoons I spent curled up on the sofa with one of his textbooks, in search of answers. I marveled at the pictures of mushroom clouds and electron configuration diagrams, trying to pronounce the words. *Valence, cation, nucleotide.*

"You think that stuff's terrific, don't you?" my mother yelled over the din of pots and pans as she started supper in the kitchen. "Give yourself time. Then you'll see that being erudite won't get you anywhere in this world. Good God," she muttered, "it's hard enough having an academic for a husband, but to have one as a daughter . . ."

Much as I loved what I read in books, I didn't like school. It was a huge, daunting place, with spiderweb hallways and too many scents of other people, too much noise and grime. Up until the point I entered school I had been used to an encapsulated universe of tasteful wallpaper and Mozart and debated aesthetics, an intimate universe in which I had to deal with the complexities of just two people. Suddenly I was thrust into a huge maze with five hundred other children from more rural, less pretentious surrounding neighborhoods who weren't like me, and not only was I expected to endure this bewildering injustice, I was also supposed to enjoy the mass herdings from classroom to cafeteria, then back again.

I resented the teachers who assumed that all children were bright-but-dumb, cheeky souls whose lives had no complexities, to be pacified by rewards of smiley faces drawn on papers and stamps on hands, to be reprimanded by a simple time-out or, in more extreme cases, a walk up the hall to the principal's office for a swat. I hated the other kids' squabbles, their stupid contests as to which homeroom lined up for lunch the straightest and quietest, thereby earning extra recess time.

Most of all, I hated the other girls in my class, whom I looked at with the same mixture of fear and longing as I did my mother. They had perky names like Becki or Mindi, little monikers with precious spellings, and wore anklets adorned by ruffles and roses and barrettes with streamers. They carried pink zippered pencil cases and monogrammed bookbags. They sat in the front row and did their work well enough to make the teachers happy, but not with such zealous perfection that they risked ostracism. They were full-lipped, saucer-eyed girls who talked incessantly of being fashion designers, interior decorators, models. They gushed. They shrieked. They traded cupcakes at lunch and braided each other's hair, exuding a pouty, flirtatious sensuality on the edge of innocence. They were flightly, but they were good girls, secure and complacent in their little circles, and I ached for their kind of careless, happy alliance.

However, a thick veil, an integument invisible to me but apparent to everyone else, separated me from them. Perhaps it was my reticence. Perhaps it was the fervor with which I threw myself into my schoolwork, as if the manipulation of numbers and the stringing together of sentences were wars won only by gold stars and excellent report cards. No matter what the reason, I was alone.

My parents argued frequently about me.

"She's gifted, Caroline," my father said. "She's lonely and starved for intellectual contact."

"She's a child, for Christ's sake!" my mother said. "I won't have her turned into a little pedant. She needs to learn that the world can be cruel to intellectuals."

"I think we should put her into private school."

"No."

"We've got the money."

"It's not an issue of money or affluence or whatever you want to make it. The fact is, she's a sensitive kid and she needs to toughen up. She needs to face facts." Something in her voice told me she wasn't ready to face the facts of her own life.

But my mother won. So I went to school and listened to the good girls giggle and I read *The History of the Atom* on the playground and came home in tears. My father would gather me into his arms and stroke my hair and whisper, "Shh, shh, angel, you've just got to bear it, but remember that you're better than them."

He told me that I shouldn't waste my time on such imbeciles, and so we remained apart, the good girls and I, the studious one with the long, dark hair who spent her days huddled over her desk. In a way it was a relief not to have to talk to anyone.

Cloying, affectionate, my father was the one who turned to me, but my mother was the person to whom I wished to turn. I feared her, that was true, but my fear was laced with a potent idolatry. She was a mulberry-and-mauve floral goddess, a Laura Ashley–clad amazon, and I desperately wanted to be close to her. Sometimes when she gave lessons, I peeked through a crack in the door and watched the tantalizing motion of her wrist as she moved the bow across the strings, and a wild fluttering resonated deep inside my chest.

I wanted to tell her to join the biggest, most famous orchestra there was. I wanted to put my arms around her neck and smell her scent of talcum powder and rosin and cologne. I wanted to run my fingers beneath her jaw and feel the angry pulse that throbbed there, but I could never get close enough, and I never dared try.

My mother's attention was a rare gift when it happened. Every once in a while she'd cancel her Saturday appointments and decide we needed an afternoon out. She'd tie a gauze scarf in her hair, grab her credit cards, and we'd drive to another small town, about an hour away from ours, whose livelihood revolved around a massive, Colonial-style complex of a department store and gallery and French restaurant. She'd turn on classical radio on the way over, and we'd have contests to see who could guess the composer of the piece first—"Debussy, no, Bartók, wait, Liszt!" we'd shout before the throaty-voiced announcer would spit out the title of the work.

Before punk came along, I never had the obsessive concern with clothes my mother did—even as an adult I was happy to live in a few simple black dresses—but on those afternoons I was so enraptured with the fact that she had devoted her whole day to me that I let her drag me by the wrist from rack to rack without comment. Much as she scoffed at "slaves of fashion," in a neatly divided world of departments and price tags she was in her element, the stylized opposite of my father and me, flourish and flair masking her anguished bitterness as she laughed and smiled and made a fool of herself. "What do you think? Is it me?" She'd bat her eyelashes comically, after she'd plunked a chartreuse wide-brimmed hat on her head and tossed a leopard-print cape around her shoulders. I'd giggle as the gray-haired salesladies stared at us in horror.

She'd try on delicate sundresses that made her look like an eighteen-year-old, and black evening gowns with heavy gold collars ("I look like fucking Nefertiti, don't I?" she'd whisper with glee), and then we'd go up to the children's section. "Do you like this?" she'd ask. "And this?" Everything I showed the slightest flicker of interest towards she'd sling over her arm, and we'd barrel into a fitting room with about ten garments over the limit.

The closest I ever came to my mother was in those locked cubicles with no space in which to turn. She didn't nag me for wadding a skirt in a heap or chastise me for fumbling with buttons the way she would have at home, and she didn't insist on critiquing how the outfit hung on me or how I had the frame of a matchstick. She'd just lean against the wall with her arms crossed, watching me out of the corner of her eye, her head turned and her expression wistful.

If I struggled with the straps on a jumper or wrestled the zipper on a dress, she'd kneel behind me and help with slow, careful fingers, and then she'd lean her chin on my shoulder and stare at our reflections in the mirror. "You know, there are people in this world who would kill for your bone structure," she'd say, and I would feel hopelessly happy.

Then we'd go get our purchases rung up; she'd shove her card across the counter at the cashier and make some remark like, "My husband'll kill me for this one," though we knew he wouldn't. Navy-and-gold plastic bags swinging in our hands, we'd run breathlessly across the street for lunch at a place that had an amazing dessert cart and required an extensive knowledge of fork etiquette. She'd order a few glasses of burgundy, enough to make her face flush, and every few minutes she'd reach over the table and squeeze my hand and say, "We should do this more often, huh?"

On the way home a cozy silence would envelop us. I'd rest my cheek against the windowpane and watch townhouses, Amish farms, identical neighborhoods slide by. She kept her gaze on the road, but there was a looseness, a sloppy calm around her which probably came from alcohol but which I attributed to contentment.

When we'd pull into the driveway, she'd stop the car, move across the seat, and draw me into her arms. "You had a good time today?" Her voice would be numb, brittle. "Yeah?"

I'd nod, head buried in the folds of her blazer.

"You love me? Do you?"

Her hand would nervously stroke my back as if it were disconnected from the rest of her body. I'd nod again.

She'd let go, move away, ready to grasp the door handle. She'd chew her lip. She'd say, "Okay."

After that we'd go inside and dart up the stairs before my father could glimpse what we got—"It's a *surprise*," we'd say in histrionic whispers—and spread all we got out on her bed. The room was enshrouded in the dim, comforting glow of early evening and the lights of her vanity mirror, and shadows flickered on the wall from the headlights of cars that turned in the cul-de-sac outside. I'd put on the new dress or skirt or sweater, and she'd French-braid my hair and let me put on her lipstick. We didn't laugh or talk or even look at each other.

When she was done making me look like I was twenty, she'd turn me around and stare into my face. She'd rest her hand against my cheek, and her eyes would blink very fast. "You're just like your father," she'd say, not with admiration or distaste, but with simple regret, as if she knew that that fact was capable of making me do something sad.

She'd smile, then, and I'd smile back, and then we'd go back downstairs, her palms on my shoulders, and I'd turn before my father in the new outfit. He'd gush his approval, and I'd keep it on all through dinner. Even when the tension came between them, I was still too happy to sense it. I wanted those evenings to go on forever.

Chapter Seven

"Sometimes I'm amazed that the world still turns," I said to Jascha one night. We sat in the chip shop across the street from the studio. We'd decided to eat supper before we tackled more of the slides. "I know that sounds solipsistic, but . . . There was an idea very popular in the Middle Ages called the correspondence theory, and what it basically said was that one man's agony could send the universe into a tailspin. You see it in Shakespeare a lot, and I've talked to my classes about it, but I never truly understood its appeal until now. Because to me, a world without Bill should spin out of control. I want floods. I want fires. I want earthquakes."

Munching on haddock, he gazed across the table at me with the same expression of alarmed curiosity I often saw on my son's face.

"I feel terrible thinking like that," I said, "but I can't help it. I walk home from work and see lights aglow in windows, and I want to scream. I imagine a million couples kissing and talking and eating tandoori in a million warm rooms above my head, and I seethe."

I looked out the window. A small girl of about seventeen walked past on the street. She had short, scraggly blond hair and wore a big beige coat. As she passed, she gazed at us wistfully. She must have thought we were lovers.

"I think one of the worst aspects of Bill's death," I said, "is that I have to face up to the nature of my love for him, the nature of our relationship when he was alive. I used to think that it was pure, the only thing of real purity in my life. To Bill, I wasn't odd or a rebel or antisocial, all those labels I'd worn before I met him."

"Isn't that what love is about? Lack of pretenses?"

"To me it is," I said. "But I can't escape this nagging feeling of . . . having used him. Of giving so little and taking so much. There was a time last fall when he came down with an infection—his immune system was weak from the drugs—and a bad fever. Not nearly as bad as the last one, but awful enough to land him in the hospital and make mortality cross my mind. He lay drenched with sweat. He twitched. He thrashed, and I held his hand. It was like pinching the string of a balloon in two fingers while it bobs wildly in the wind. Do you know what I said to him? I said, 'You sure as hell better not die on me, honey, because if you do I'll go even crazier than I am now.' Oh, I meant it as a joke, and he took it as one. Laughed in the midst of his fire. But to think that I didn't offer words of comfort, words of reassurance—that I was too worried about how I'd go on if he left me. . . ."

"That was a legitimate worry."

"You sound like him," I said. "Always humoring me. 'Oh, no, love, nothing wrong with that, burn the house down if it'll make you feel better.' "

"Damn right I'm humoring you. If I don't, there won't be a retrospective."

I laughed. "You have no fear of telling it like it is, do you?"

"I see no reason to tell it otherwise."

I toyed with a chip on my plate. "And then there was the matter of Australia," I said. "As long as I could remember, Bill had been attracted to aboriginal culture, the whole Dreamtime concept. For years he fantasized about going into the bush. We seriously considered a trip, but we had Curran and not much money. When he was in the hospital last fall, when there was some question as to whether or not he'd come out, I told him, 'Bill, you make it through this, and I'll take you to Australia, I promise.'

"Well, he made it, but we never went. It would've been a stupid move on our part, anyway; what if he got sick while we were there? But I never tried. Never looked into the cost of plane tickets, or an itinerary. Eight years he held me together, and I couldn't even call a damn travel agent about a vacation in Australia."

"I think you're beating yourself over the head for crimes you didn't commit," Jascha said.

"Of course I am," I said. "This guilt over a spoken sentence and a broken promise is stupid. A soothing word or a trip wouldn't have saved him. But after he's gone . . ."

I sighed.

"I don't know how to explain Bill and me," I said. "I don't know if language exists to explain us." With him I had a feeling of absolute *knowing*. Not the cliché of lovers-as-one who finish each other's sentences, but the sensation that Bill's gestures exploded from my hands, that I'd stepped into his body as easily as I'd walk through a rice curtain. He was my elixir, my addiction. I knew it was perverse to think of the man I loved as a drug, but it was true. He sang in my bloodstream. He touched me, and I was lulled. He coaxed the words onto my silent tongue. You get loved like that, and you're bound to become selfish. You're bound to wonder how you'll survive when that love's gone."

Jascha leaned forward, napkin in hand. "Hold still," he said. "You've got ketchup on the side of your mouth. Let me get it."

His thumb brushed my cheek. Under the table, I dug my fingernails into my palms. I clenched my teeth so I wouldn't cry out. I knew it was silly, that he wasn't Bill no matter how gentle his fingers were, but still my shell-shocked body pined for hands to slide down my arms and awaken me with their firm touch.

He said, "Let's get back to work, shall we?"

. . .

We walked across the street and settled into our dim, musty room. I took off my shoes and sat on the couch with my knees drawn up and my arms encircling them, my skirt spread around me. My stomach churned with dread as Jascha joined me, as slide by slide we advanced out of the bright, carefree years and into the last few months of my husband's life.

"The next painting is incredible," he said. "It's the best piece of his I've seen."

Noticing the date of completion scrawled in the lower right corner of the slide, I gasped. "He never showed me this."

On the screen, dark, murky colors reminiscent of Munch glared at us. In the foreground of the painting gnarled, sinister black hands pulled Bill down into a greenish-brown grave as his mouth contorted into a scream. On the far left stood Curran and I, dressed in black. I glowered, shoulders hunched, my too-red lips drawn back in a possessive snarl as I clutched Curran to me, my too-long fingernails grazing his small waist. He ducked his head against my shoulder in the hope of escape, but with my free hand I kept his face turned towards the horror, ignoring his eyes glazed with fright.

"Oh, God, Bill," I said.

"Not a very flattering portrait, is it?" Jascha asked.

"No," I said, "but it might be a true one if I'm not careful."

"What do you mean?"

"I've seen grief flatten a marriage," I said. "I've seen it subvert the way a parent looks at his child. I don't want that to happen to me as a mother. I can't let it happen."

He gestured towards the painting. "Why portray you like this, then?"

"There's always the desire," I said.

"What desire?"

"To chicken out. To give up that creed every mother follows, the one that says, Be strong, be strong at any cost. Put your son's needs and your son's pain ahead of your own, even if your own threatens to swallow you. Find his mittens for him, cook him his favorite supper, help him with his homework, when what you really want is to drop to your knees and bawl."

"Are you afraid you'll chicken out?"

"Terribly. I always have been."

"Did Bill realize that?"

"Until I saw this painting, I didn't think so," I said. "He was so oblivious, you know? Oblivious to a fault. He slept through thunderstorms, while I lay there in the dark and watched the curtains billow, the lightning flash.

"Right after Curran was born, I'd burst into tears all the time. Bill would sit beside me and stroke my back. 'What's wrong, love?' he'd ask, and I'd say, 'Nothing . . . now.' He'd laugh. 'Well, then, what have you got to cry about?' That's how he was. Cheerful. Naive. Forgetting that light throws shadows. I could never make him understand that it was the future I wept for, the wrong things that could happen later."

"But he saw the future, what could happen, and painted it here."

"Yes," I said softly. "Yes, he did."

"Gloria, do you mind if we use this? Would it bother you?"

"No," I said. "Go ahead."

"You're sure?"

"I'm sure."

"Let me check the title on it," he said, and leaned over to skim his list. "Here we go. *Necessary Madness.*"

"*Necessary Madness,*" I repeated.

"Yeah. I wonder what that's supposed to mean."

"Self-preservation," I said. "When you're drowning, you'll clutch anything. Because you have to. You have no other choice."

"Even if it's madness?" he asked. "Even if your very effort to survive might make you lose your grip?"

"Even then."

By the time I got home it was ten o'clock. I found Mrs. Romdourl on the living-room sofa, reading in the lamplight.

"He went to bed about half an hour ago," she said.

"How was he?"

"Fine."

"Did he do his homework?"

"Without my even asking."

I took a ten-pound note from my purse and handed it to her.

"Oh, no," she said. "I can't take this. Save it for yourself."

"Don't argue with me, Deepa," I said. "You give far too much of your time to me to go unrewarded."

She smiled and patted my arm, then left. I slipped into Curran's room and sat beside him on the bed. He slept on his stomach, one elbow and one knee hanging off the mattress's edge, breath sticky. In the glow of the night-light shaped like a sailboat,

I gazed at him and remembered myself as a twenty-three-year-old who had just been handed seven pounds of new life wrapped in a blue blanket dotted with bunnies, who had cradled his skull in her cupped palms, stared into his primitive, sapphire-colored eyes, and shaken with the burden. I remembered Bill, who'd sat beside me on the bed, his arm around both of us. Euphoria and amazement captured his face when Curran gripped his finger. "Wow, oh, *wow*," he'd said.

And we had given him his own name. No litanies for the dead. No entrapment the way I had been trapped, not even out of reverence.

Now I watched my son's translucent eyelids flutter, and heard him sigh in sleep. Gently I turned his wrist over and ran my fingertip down his milky-blue, unblemished vein. How easy it would be to furrow his pale, downy brows with confusion, to feed him my agony disguised as sugary icing, to seduce him into rebellion.

Chapter Eight

When I exploded into adolescence, I felt like a walking bomb, a tangled mess of too-long arms and legs and stark hungers. The idea of having a catty legion of friends to gossip and fight and try on eyeshadow at drugstore makeup counters with struck me as anathema to my whole being. When I walked through the halls at school with my hair raked into a hurried topknot and with a leather knapsack stuffed full of compulsively neat notes slung over one shoulder, lost in the labryinth of varsity sports banners and locker-openers' chatter, I was convinced that I'd been tattooed with a million epithets of difference, their indelible marks glistening, stamped on my skin: *dark, weird, crazy.* I was bones when the universe demanded flesh; black turtlenecks and ripped jeans when the watchwords were soft sweaters and vivid skirts, shakily cerebral in the face of the comfortably visceral.

My father said, "Don't worry about it, love. You're ahead of your time. You're perceptive."

My mother said, "Why don't you join Student Council?"

He got me through Honors geometry with an A; she invited bubbly, vacuous girls to sleep over in an attempt to get me a social life. Those terrible evenings, I cringed at the sound of the doorbell, while she glided in a classy column dress and pumps across the polished wood floor of the foyer to let in bitch after bitch who squealed with amazement at how huge our house was and ran up and down the spiral staircase all night, making microwave popcorn and bouncing on the guest bed. Under the guise of brushing my teeth, I'd lock myself in the bathroom and listen to them argue over who was the hottest guy in British Literature class while I stared at my pale face and longed to smash the mirror.

After the next day's breakfast, though, it would all be over, their slouch socks and nightshirts and overnight bags picked up off my bedroom floor, their cereal bowls cleared from the sink. My mother would swish smugly around the kitchen and hum, pleased with herself for being such an attentive mother. "Wasn't that fun?" she'd ask.

"That was a farce," I'd say, "and you know it."

Her face would crumple, and before she could protest I'd

storm down the hall. My father's study would be cloaked with the golden glow of a Sunday morning. He'd look up from his desk, motion all five feet eight inches of me onto the edge of his chair, and slip his arm around me. "So have the banshees left us?"

"Hopefully forever," I said with a laugh. "No more comparative studies of every high school male within a fifty-mile radius."

He smiled. "And who was deemed most worthy in your opinion?"

I leaned my head against his shoulder. He stroked back a lock of my hair. I could feel him breathing. The loneliness fell from me easily as water. "None of them," I said.

When I was fourteen, punk came out. Suddenly subversion was validated. I bought the boots, the chains, the rags. I painted my fingernails black and cut my hair and dyed it so that in the light it glimmered purple. I joined the school radio station, headed by anarchists, and during our meetings in the lecture room after class, we'd sit on tables and make out playlists while listening to the Clash, agonizing over the need for revolt, and discussing how one could tell a person's political affiliation by the color shoelaces he wore in his Doc Martens. We threw basement parties which lasted until all hours.

Amazingly, throughout this I still managed to keep a perfect grade-point average. After station meetings, I'd get one of the members who had a car to drop me off at my father's college, and I'd do research for history papers in the library until his final class of the day let out. He'd find me seated on a couch with my black leather feet propped on a glass table, my face buried be-hind a *Rolling Stone* or *Newsweek* once I had finished my aca-demic reading.

Then we'd drive downtown to an Italian restaurant we liked, which had teal-colored walls and fresh flowers on each table. As she handed us our plates of linguine with shrimp marinara, the waitress would stare at us, the gray-haired father with a Shetland wool cardigan draped around his shoulders and the sullen daugh-ter in the garish plaid skirt and fishnet stockings. While I de-voured a slice of rum cake, my father would stroke my free hand and tell me stories about his colleague's pregnant sixteen-year-old daughter. "You know that I'll support you no matter what deci-sions you make," he said, his pale, gentle eyes daring me to do something bad.

Every time I stayed out late, he met me at the door and led me upstairs, arm slung around my shoulders, finger against my lips to silence my thick-tongued laughter. He sat on my bedroom carpet and helped me with my Latin homework at two a.m. When I got drunk, his soft hands held my skull steady over the bathroom sink as I retched, and when my knees wobbled down onto the tile, he picked me up and carried me into bed, pulling back the sheets with one hand and laying me on the mattress.

"I'll tell your mother it was something you ate," he said. I nodded, my throat still in burn from the vodka, the lyrics to "An-archy in the U.K." floating through my brain as fitfully I dreamed of England. He bowed his head, folded my fingers over, and pressed my knuckles to his mouth. I knew he was thinking of Adrienne.

• • •

My junior year I started going out with Mike, a senior and fellow radio station member, who wore a studded leather jacket and had spiky, bleached hair. He had been kicked out of three private schools, and lived down the street from me, in a lovely old Victorian house. Unlike me, however, he had sweet, unassuming parents.

One night in December, I walked over to visit him when his family was out shopping. We sat on the green camelback sofa in his living room. I stared at the candles on the Christmas tree, and their soft light stirred in me a thousand apologies, a longing for home. He lit a cigarette, took a drag, and passed it to me. I inhaled and tried not to cry.

"You're lucky," I said. "Six more months and you'll be out of here."

"Not if I don't pass Advanced Comp."

"Well, if you aren't so fucking stubborn and let me proofread for you, maybe you will."

He laughed. Turned my chin to face him. "You're a madwoman," he said.

I moved closer so that my knees touched his. I put my hands on his shoulders and dug my fingernails into his neck. "Mike," I said softly. "I'm scared of myself."

"You shouldn't be," he said, and pressed his mouth to mine. By some voracious reflex, I slid back and unbuttoned my skirt. We dropped to the floor. My spine stung as I hit the rug. I grabbed fistfuls of his shirt. His zipper rasped against my bare skin. I bit my lip. Tasted blood. His face swam above my head as he shoved himself inside me.

Afterwards, he leaned down and kissed me roughly on the neck. I rose and put my clothes back on, and then we stood at the kitchen counter and ate his mother's Russian tea cookies as if it had been nothing, numb, defiant.

That night I walked home with my black wool duster coat clutched around me. The sidewalk and the road shone with a dusting of snow, and lights glowed in each house I passed. I thought again of Adrienne, Adrienne who in her white beret had glistened on the quad at Oxford on a night like this. I balled my fingers into fists. I'm not her, I told myself. I'm not that pure, intellectual darling.

I let myself into the house and made it halfway up the stairs when I heard my father call. "Gloria? Is that you?"

"Yeah, Dad." Sighing, I came back down and stood in the doorway of his study. "I'm home."

He set aside his stack of chem labs. "I was worried," he said. "I didn't know where you were."

"I'm sorry. I just went down to Mike's."

"You didn't tell me."

"I told Mom. She was in the middle of a lesson, so she probably forgot. She said it was okay as long as I came back by ten."

"But I didn't know."

"For Christ's sake, Dad, I said I was sorry! At sixteen you don't think I have the autonomy to walk a block away from you? Or is it fine to run off if it's our little secret, but if my mother's involved, forget it?"

He motioned me inside. I sat beside him and rested my head on my arms on his desk. I felt sticky, wrung-out. "What's wrong, love?" he asked.

He reached out and gently stroked my hair. It was such a simple action, but it felt more painful than thrashing to the floor with Mike had.

I said, "I don't know."

One night that winter, Mike dropped me off and, warm with liquor, I stumbled up the slick, icy front walk. Fashionable though they were, my combat boots had miserable traction, and I fell flat on my face on the porch. I crawled on my hands and knees to the door, grabbed the knob to pull myself up, and fumbled for my house key. It wasn't there. I rang the bell. My mother answered, her floral silk robe wrinkled, her hair rumpled for once.

"Get in here," she said. "Now."

I stepped inside and slumped to the floor.

"You're drunk," she said. "You're rip-roaring drunk, aren't you?"

"Of course not, Mommy," I slurred. "I've got complete and utter control of my mental faculties, can't you see that?"

She grabbed my wrist and dragged me to my feet.

"Look at yourself," she said.

I stared down. Blood from a gash on my chin dripped onto my Sex Pistols T-shirt and the black turtleneck I wore under it. My nylons had ripped, and the skin was torn on both my knees.

"Come on," she said, and led me into the bathroom. "It is two-thirty in the morning, two-thirty in the fucking morning, Gloria Merchant, and I really don't appreciate this."

She sat me down on the toilet seat and rummaged through the medicine cabinet. "We might as well start with your chin. Jesus. How'd you do this to yourself?"

"Fell," I mumbled. I leaned back against the wall and closed my eyes.

"Don't fall asleep on me, damn it." She held my head still as she bandaged my chin. "You'll live, but not without a scar, I'll bet."

She knelt down and dabbed my knees. I winced at the peroxide's sting. "Yes, I know it hurts," she said, "but maybe you ought to think about that next time before you try to down the whole bottle, hmm?"

I nodded.

"Revolt." She stood and put the peroxide and the box of bandages back in the cabinet, slamming the door. "I never had a chance for any goddamned revolt."

I staggered to my feet. She shoved me back down and put her hands on my shoulders. "Wait, I'm not done with you yet," she said.

I stared up into her blurry face.

"Listen," she said, "your father may let you get away with this shit, but I won't. You are too intelligent to do this to yourself. I don't ever, ever want to see you like this again. Do you hear me?"

"Yes," I whispered.

"You can whine at me all you like about my being the bitch of all bitches, but that won't change the fact that I love you and won't let you wreck your life." She hauled me up. "Now I want to get upstairs and go to bed."

She went into the kitchen for a glass of water, and I crept into my father's study. I turned on the banker's lamp, went to the bookshelf, and took down the B volume of the encyclopedia. I turned to the page with Robert Browning, and there Adrienne lay, smiling softly at me. "You idiot," I said. "You didn't have to drive to Manchester for the weekend. You could have stayed with him."

I laid the book down and searched through the desk drawer for a pair of scissors. When I found them, I sat cross-legged on the floor with the photograph and hacked away at Adrienne until she was a mess of black-and-white strips.

"Gloria," my mother said from the doorway, "what the hell are you doing? I told you to get to bed."

She came inside and sat before me.

"Sweetheart," she said, "why are you crying?"

I looked up. My mouth twisted with sobs. Salt spilled down my cheeks.

"Oh, God," I said. "He'll kill me. I've got to put it back together."

With one arm she pulled me against her and kissed my forehead. "I'll help you," she said. We sat there on the floor for an hour, silent, our hands touching as we used up a whole roll of Scotch tape repairing his idol.

Chapter Nine

One Friday night I stood at the stove, stirring a pot of stew, watching the potatoes and carrots as they swirled to the motion of my wrist, and I thought: I have kept my promise. I am neither a Riordan nor a Caroline. I respect my son's youth. I iron my blouses, but don't mind if they wrinkle. I wear mascara, but don't hyperventilate if it runs. I experience loss, but I still function.

I hummed as I set out two bowls, two spoons, and two napkins. In the living room, Curran laughed at some banal show on television. *You hear that?* I asked myself. That soft, sweet, high-pitched laughter of a child? He is yours, but he is not you. He is intelligent and inquisitive, but he does not read chemistry textbooks or come home in tears. Of course he's grieving, inside he aches, but he will be fine, and you have done well, do you hear? You have done well. . . .

I returned to the stove and gave the stew a final stir. Too hard, I realized, because the next thing I knew, the pot tipped and clattered to the floor, drenching me and the linoleum, and it was Friday night in the city I'd grown to love, and the flat was swollen with warmth, and Bill was not in my arms.

"Curran!" I screamed. "Curran, help me!"

He rushed into the kitchen. He put out his hand to stop me, but I skidded to the floor, slamming my back against the oven. Pain knocked the breath from me. I sat there, stunned, soaked amongst vegetables, and began to cry. I put my hands over my face as the sobs ripped me.

"Mum? Are you okay?"

I lifted my head. Bit my lip. Reached out my hands. "Come here, baby," I whispered. He knelt beside me. I saw stains from the splattered broth on his jeans when he shifted, and they made me cry harder.

"Don't worry," he said. "I can help you clean up."

"No, no, you don't have to, angel," I said. "Just hold me. Please, please, please just hold me."

He put his arms, his tiny little arms, around me. "Tighter," I whispered. He hugged me so hard my ribs hurt. He kissed my burning forehead.

"Mum, I'm hungry," he said.

"I know you are, sweetheart," I said. Snot trickled from my nose down to my mouth. On the television, an audience roared with laughter.

I closed my eyes and sent silent messages to my son: Your chromosomes are one-half composed of the penchants and desires and scents and hopes and superstitions of your father, the man I shared a bed with, but you are not him. And I won't expect you to be. I'll never hurt you. And I said that, "I'll never hurt you," into his ear, on the kitchen floor, over and over, as if repeating the words like a mantra would keep me from doing it, from hurting him.

After a while he untangled himself from me, and as he retreated into the bathroom, I heard his footsteps and then the delicious sound of running water. He came back and sponged my flushed face with a wet washcloth. "Thank you so much," I said.

I was on my hands and knees, scrubbing the last splotches of stew off the floor, when the doorbell rang. Curran called, "It's Jascha!"

"Jesus, Mary, and Leopold Bloom," I said, and grabbed the counter to pull myself to my feet.

"Another chaotic dinner?" Jascha asked.

"You could say that," I said. "Seeing as I'm wearing it."

"I just came by to get your approval on the final list of paintings," he said, "but why don't I take you both out?"

"Could you?" He nodded. "You're sweet. Thanks."

"No problem."

"Give me a minute to change, and I'll be ready."

I went into my bedroom and pulled on jeans and a big black sweater. In the kitchen I heard Curran ask, "You're a sculptor? Are you really?" I glimpsed myself—red-eyed, swollen-faced—in the mirror, and scowled at the woman I realized I'd never been before.

We ate cheap sandwiches at a coffeehouse near the university, and then walked up and down the familiar streets from my college days: Leigh, Gower. I pointed out places to them. "See that café? I used to waitress there."

"I can't imagine you waiting on *anybody*," Jascha said.

"I did, though," I said. "Worked illegally. Got tons of free food. Oh—that pub over there, the one with the patio on the roof, was where we all got drunk after finals."

I thought of the pub's dimness, its chattering voices, the smell of ale on breath and skin. And me, sick of *de rigueur* nonconformity yet clinging to it like a life raft, on the far edge of belonging.

Next to Jascha and Curran, bundled in my coat, I wondered how passersby saw us. Windblown, out for a walk in the crisp air on a cold February evening, a dark-haired couple, fashionably casual, and their solemn blond son. I jammed my hands into my pockets and pretended that it was the truth.

We took the tube back to my flat. Jascha sat in the kitchen while I put Curran to bed. He looked small and wan, propped up on his pillows. "Tonight," he said, "when we went out and you showed us all the old places where you and Dad used to go, I wanted him to be with us so much that . . . well, this is daft, but I imagined that Jascha was Dad—I mean, I know he's not, he's lots different, but I just thought maybe I'd feel better . . ."

"I know, love."

"The thing was, I *did.* And I felt bad then because it wasn't right. It wasn't right for me to be happy when Dad's gone and you're so sad."

"No, Curran. Listen to me," I said. "It's perfectly all right. You don't have to worry about me or Dad. If you're happy, well, you just scream out the window and tell the world that you are at two in the morning, if you feel like it."

He giggled. "Can I really?"

"Well, not at two in the morning. We don't want to wake Mrs. Romdourl." I leaned down and kissed him.

"You still smell of vegetables," he said.

I went back into the kitchen and with a sigh slumped into a chair across from Jascha. "Something tells me you're bothered by more than just the fact that tonight you dumped half of Sainsbury's fruit and veg on yourself," he said.

"Damn it," I said, "why do you always insist on making me laugh when I want to cry?"

" 'Excess of sorrow laughs; excess of joy weeps.' "

"Blake."

"Could you stop being the English teacher for a second?"

"What's that supposed to mean?"

"That if you'd quit analyzing every move you made and every one you contemplate, as if your life's a piece of poetry to be explicated, maybe you'd feel better."

I stared down at my nails. I'd bitten them down to nubs.

Loneliness generates bad habits. In the past few weeks, I'd begun to smoke again, something I hadn't done since I was a teenager. I gnawed my lip and the skin around my fingers until they bled. Voracious. Bill had been like that, those last few months he was still energetic. He'd come up behind me as I washed dishes, run his hands through my hair, grab great fistfuls, graze his mouth against my ear, his breath hot, as if he knew he had to get his senses full of me before the end.

"Gloria?"

"Yeah?"

"I've got the list made up if you want to see it."

"Okay."

He slid the list across the table. I read over his selections.

"I've got no problem with what's here," I said. "My qualms mostly lie with your presentation."

"There'll be no unnecessary hype. Just the necessary madnesses."

"That wasn't funny, Jascha."

"I know it wasn't. I'm sorry."

I rubbed my forehead. "When I had my little culinary disaster," I said, "I sort've snapped. This front I've been keeping up fell from me like the pot did off the stove. And Curran, poor thing, came in and said, 'Mum, I'll help you clean it up.' He sat down on the floor and held me. He put a wet rag to my bloated, fevered face and told me not to worry, when he should have been in the other room watching cartoons and waiting for me to bring his supper on a tray.

"But it's so easy to do without Bill here to ground me. It's so easy to say, 'Darling, make Mummy a sandwich for supper, she feels awful right now,' to say, 'Come here, give me a hug, I've had a rotten day.' The other night I said to him, 'Curran, we *are* going to get through this, aren't we?' He looked at me and he said, 'Mum, I don't know.' "

"Don't you think you're blaming yourself too much? He seems pretty well-adjusted to me."

"Sure he does. He goes to school, he plays video games with his friend who lives downstairs. Maybe he's a bit quieter, a bit more pensive lately, but he's always been that way. He just scares me. . . . The grief of a child is so buried. It pops up in the softest, most incongruous moments. Like tonight. As I was tucking him in, he said that he felt ashamed to be happy when I'm sad like this. Do you know what that feels like, to know that your son can't be happy because of you?"

I thought of Louise lecturing him in the kitchen after Bill's funeral: *You're the man of the house now, and you mustn't mind if your mum gets a bit mental.*

"You're his mother," Jascha said. "Of course he wants to help you. Of course he wants you to be happy when he is."

"But there are too many fine lines," I said, "and I've never been one for tightrope-walking."

I didn't tell him that Curran had pretended he was Bill, or that I'd walked with my fists stuffed in my pockets all night so I wouldn't reach for his hand, or that I'd wanted to simply because I didn't feel right walking the university streets, the streets of the early days with Bill, without someone's fingers laced through mine.

Chapter Ten

I graduated second in my high school class, which meant that I had the distinction of being the school's first purple-haired salutatorian. At commencement I gave a speech about the importance of individuality in a turbulent world. My father wept. My mother complained about the stadium's heat.

I went on to major in English at a small, liberal college in New York with a reputation for being too artsy and sexually perverse for its own good. While there, I mellowed a bit. I grew my hair and let it fade back to its natural color. I kept my affinity for combat boots, but also developed one for long, gauzy skirts. "I am surrounded by erudite people," I wrote to my father. "I even have deep conversations in cafés and coffeehouses with some of them, but I still can't shake my feelings of apartness."

My senior year, I got accepted into a foreign-exchange program in London. My father drove up to see me before I left. He sat on the edge of my bed and watched me with a desolate look on his face while I packed jeans and heavy sweaters.

"My God," he said, gesturing towards the textbooks and clothes and pizza delivery boxes on the floor. "Caroline would go absolutely barmy if she saw this place."

"Why didn't she come with you?"

"Lessons. She had lessons."

"Right. I should've remembered her selfless dedication to scaring the shit out of poor, defenseless little fourth-graders so they'll play in tune."

"Gloria. It's better that she's not here. That way we can talk in peace." He grinned.

"But she could've tried. She could've given up one damn afternoon."

The door swung open. It was Beth, my roommate. Her cropped hair stood up in tiny green spikes, and she wore a T-shirt that said FUCK ART, LET'S KILL. My father twittered. For a moment I was embarrassed, ashamed of him, even, that gaunt, stoop-shouldered man who sat surrounded by Cure posters.

"You're leaving already?" Beth asked.

"My flight's at two."

"Are you excited?"

I nodded. "Beth," I said, "this is my father, Riordan Merchant."

He extended his hand. "Hello, Beth," he said. "I must tell you, my dear, that I've had a secret desire for hair like yours for years, but I've also a wife who'd slap me with a messy divorce if I ever tried to emulate it."

Beth smiled. "Well, in that case, I'd stick with the color you've got."

"You don't know my mother," I said. "Tell him to go for your hair, Beth."

They both laughed. "We'd best be off," my father said.

I turned to Beth. "I guess I'm out of here," I said. She held out her arms, and we hugged. We hadn't been that close—we'd only been roommates for a month—but I was seized with one of the short, intense bursts of sentimentality I always felt when faced with the kindnesses of those who I'd thought cared nothing.

"You've got to write to me and tell me all about your exploits with those British men," Beth said.

"What's this about British men?" my father asked.

Beth giggled. "Your father is so cute, Gloria," she whispered in my ear. "He looks like Anthony Hopkins. And he's charming."

"Yeah, well, he's my father," I said.

On the way to the airport, he and I were silent. It was only when we sat waiting for my flight to be called that the words came.

"You don't know how much I want to go along," my father said.

"Why? To be with me or go to London?"

"Both."

"Come with me, then."

"I think they just announced your flight," he said.

We stood. He had tears in his eyes as he took my hands.

"Promise you'll write me," we said in unison.

"Owe me a beer," I said.

He laughed. "When Caroline's not looking, that is. But seriously, love, you will write, won't you?"

"Of course. I'll be writing you the second I'm in the air. You know that."

"And ring me up as soon as you get the phone number to your flat."

I nodded. "I'd better go."

He put his arms around me and stood there with his chin on top of my head.

"Dad," I said, "if you don't let go of me right now, I'm going to miss my plane."

He drew back. "Sorry."

"Don't look so sad," I said, and leaned up to kiss his hollow cheek. It was the last time I would see him alive.

I lived in a big, bare flat on Leigh Street, near the university, with three other girls: Meg, an actress who wore too much eyeliner and high heels with jeans; Sarah, a delicate mystic who played guitar and burned scented candles; and Pandora, a fellow American, with dyed red hair and a wicked laugh, who'd changed her name from Rebecca out of principle. While not at class, we lounged around playing with Ouija boards and debating Marxist versus liberal feminism. "I'm intoxicated with the city, with its grayness," I wrote to my father. "As for my own . . . I don't know."

One weekend Pan suggested we go down to Chelsea and see an artists' co-op a friend of hers was in. It was a huge, minimalist place with harsh lighting and hardwood floors, but the others gushed over it as Nick, the cropped-haired friend with an earring, led them on a tour, showing them quasi-African sculptures and "postmodernist" pottery. I sat on the windowsill in my boots and a long black dress and cardigan, shivering.

The front door swung open with a gust of leaves and night air. A man came in wearing an old field coat and a pair of loafers whose stitching was almost shot. He waved to some people who milled in the studio, gave a perfunctory nod to Pan and the girls, and sat on the floor beneath me as if he'd known me my entire life.

"Bill Burgess," he said, and offered his hand.

"Gloria Merchant," I said. "You work here?"

"Yeah," he said, stretching out his legs. "But I try not to have pretensions about it."

"So you're not into those 'dysfunctional double boilers' or whatever Nick said those pieces of scrap metal are over there?"

He grinned. "God, no. My paintings and I are disgustingly normal."

I tipped my head back and laughed. "I'm glad."

"I take it you despise pretension, too?"

"I do . . . but that doesn't mean I'm not living pretentiously."

He gestured towards Pandora and Meg and Sarah. "You mean in their kind of way?"

"Exactly," I said. "They're great girls. Terrific fun. But I'm not like them. I'm a loner, I guess."

"By choice?" he asked.

"I don't think so," I said. "Although I may make my loneliness worse."

"Nothing wrong with solitude," he said. "Until you find that person, the one who accepts, who understands."

I pulled my cardigan in tighter.

"Say," he said, "you look cold. Want some coffee?"

He led me into a small, grungy kitchen. The fluorescent strip of light above the sink hummed. I blinked at the brightness, remembering Adrienne, seeing her again in my mind, her features terrified blossoms in the headlights. I thought of myself as a sad, pitiful girl trying too hard to be rebellious, as a child who fought to brush away her father's tears before they fell. I leaned against the counter and drank my coffee, feeling ashamed as I gazed at Bill over the rim of my mug.

"Better?" he asked.

I nodded. Set the saucer on the Formica. We reached for each other at the same time, cueless. I rested my chin on his shoulder. He ran his hand over my back. We could hear someone chiseling away at a block of marble in the studio. I closed my eyes and imagined it was me he was shaping.

After a few soft moments, we pulled apart. He didn't smile or speak. I wanted to pull him back against my flesh, breathe him into me.

"Gloria?" Meg called from the main space. "Are you coming?"

I turned my head. "Give me a goddamned minute, would you?" I yelled.

He laughed under his breath. Then, filled with purpose again, he pulled a piece of paper off a message pad by the phone, dug a pen from a stash in an empty coffee jar on the counter, and wrote down his number. The motion of his hand seemed to take a millennium, but the digits came out in a broad scrawl. He handed the slip of paper to me, folded my fingers over. There was no hint of smugness or even expectation, on his face. Only pure offering.

We turned and walked back to the studio. The girls stood before me with Nick: coy Sarah in her batik dress, high-cheekboned Meg in her tunic and miniskirt, and Pan just Pan with her ripped jeans and messy hair.

"So what were you doing with Bill Burgess in the kitchen?" she chirped on the way home.

"Drinking coffee and no more," I said. "Get your mind out of the gutter."

That night I went straight to my room without saying another word. I crawled into my pajamas and into bed before anyone could entice me into a Tarot card session or an impromptu drink round. Through the wall I heard the sounds of pillows flying, shrieks, a lamp knocked over. I lay still, hollow yet satisfied. Moonlight bloomed a lush shadow on my upraised palm.

• • •

I called him a week later. I got one of his roommates first. Then there was the sound of the television and running water and finally his voice. "Hey," he said. "I was wondering when you'd ring."

"I didn't want to bother you," I said.

"Well, you aren't bothering me," he said. "Come over for dinner. It's a grotty madhouse, but one of my mates makes a dead good boil-in-bag curry."

I laughed. I couldn't help it. It was his voice, that voice so casual and yet so earnest, making me buoyant.

"What?" he said. "Have you seen a particularly amusing side of curry I haven't?"

"No," I said. "In fact, I love it. And I live in a grotty madhouse, too. But I wouldn't mind seeing yours."

I went over that night. The flat was in Earl's Court, small and dark and dingier than mine. We sat in the kitchen as the curry boiled. The room was tiny and yellow, with overgrown plants hanging in the bay window and an ugly plastic cloth on the table, but as the darkness closed in around us and steam rose in the pot on the stove, a drowsy warmth surged through my veins.

"So where's the marvelous mate-who's-a-chef?" I asked.

"At the co-op."

"Do you always kick your roommates out when you've got a girl over?"

He laughed. "There haven't been that many."

"Oh, come on. A nice boy like you."

We took our bowls of curry into the living room and sat on a ratty brown corduroy sofa. We talked about art and our futures and the subtle madnesses of our parents and the insincerity of people. Soon it was ten-thirty.

"Damn," I said. "I promised Sarah that tonight I'd help her study for her philosophy exam."

We stood, and he walked me to the door and handed me my coat. I put it on. "It's been lovely," he said.

He reached out his arms and drew me into them. I lifted my head, and he smudged his lips across my mouth. I ran my fingers through his unkempt brown hair and darted urgent kisses along his jaw. I shrugged out of my coat and let it fall to the floor.

"I thought you had to help one of your flatmates revise," he whispered.

"She can wait," I said, and buried my face in his neck.

Towards morning, in a bed that wasn't mine, I woke to the sound of rain. I lay there and stared at the outline of Bill's back and thought, *This is gorgeous, but it won't last long.* I wanted to lift myself up with my palms and lean over to kiss his broad, slumbering mouth, but I must have fallen back asleep before I could do it, because when I opened my eyes again he was curled beside me, shoulder pressed to mine, and the rain had grown into a fullfledged storm, the windows were rattling with thunder.

Those days I was stupid with happiness. On Saturdays we went to the Tate and marveled at the Hockney paintings in the gallery, then ate seedcake in the restaurant downstairs, each time trying to find something new on the mural of Epicurania. I tried not to think about the wild, despairing timbre which colored my father's latest letters.

"I've committed emotional manslaughter," he wrote. "I'm not what your mother wants, she's not what I need. What I need is gone, gone, and all I'm doing is hurting everyone else, making them into replacements for her. . . ."

One evening he phoned me while I was at Bill's. I took the call in the bedroom. Bill lay there and grinned at me.

"Dad," I said. "Hi."

"I've been trying to reach you for days, but you've been out."

"I've been pretty busy."

"A girl gave me the number of where you are now when I rang your flat. Meg, she said her name was."

"Meg. Yeah."

"How have you been?"

"Terrific. I've got a lot of friends."

"And your studies are brilliant as usual, I hope."

"I wouldn't call them that, but I'm doing all right. It's tougher here."

"I told you it would be."

Bill sat up and leaned against my back. He toyed with my hair.

"Gloria? Are you still there?"

"I'm still here, Dad."

"I miss you terribly."

Bill brushed his lips against my neck.

"I miss you, too. Is Mom being her usual self?"

"Unfortunately. Friday-night dinner parties with histrionics over whether the rose-colored candles match the mauve table-cloth. Gloria, I just don't know what I'm going to do. I . . ."

While he rambled I tossed the phone into the air and caught it in my hands a few times. Bill burst out laughing. "Shut up," I said, and clamped my hand over his mouth. "No, no, not you, Dad. Bill's just being incorrigible."

"Who's Bill?"

"The artist I met in Chelsea. I told you about him. Don't you remember?"

"Oh. Yes. Bill."

"Listen, Dad, I've really got to go," I said. "I'll talk to you later."

"You were nice," Bill said when I hung up. "Do you always treat your own father with such callousness?"

"No," I said. "In fact, I've catered to him for the last twenty-one years. I think it's time I stopped."

He smiled. "Come here."

Later, staring up at the ceiling, I thought: It's come full circle. Here I am, just like my mother, on my back on a bed in a disheveled flat in Earl's Court, with a gentle, delicious-voiced man above me.

Chapter Eleven

When I went to pick up Curran at Deepa's after work one night, I found the usually noisy flat draped in a guarded hush. Raj, who was eight, answered the door. "Curran's in the lounge," he said, somber-voiced, and jerked his thumb in my son's direction.

Curran sat on the Romdourls' tweed sofa, head in his hands. Deepa sat at his side with her arm around him. "Your mum's here," she said.

He looked up. His left eye was blackened.

"Please don't be mad at me," he said.

"There was a fight at school," Deepa whispered. "A note from the teacher's in his bag, explaining it."

"Come on," I said to him. "We'll go home and talk about this."

Upstairs, in the kitchen, I read the note and sighed as Curran ran down the hall and slammed the door to his room. I waited until I heard the creak of the bedsprings before I went in and sat next to him. I stroked his back.

"Want to tell me what happened?"

"Why should I? You read all about it." His words were muffled by the pillow.

"Mrs. Cunningham didn't give me your side of the story."

He lifted his head, and I winced at the sight of the dark streaks that radiated from his eye like the rays of a cruel sun. "We were outside," he said. "It was almost time to come in for Maths, and I was standing against the wall, talking to Raj, doing nothing to vex anyone, really. All of a sudden, Nigel Clark—he's in the fifth form, he's massive, and he always teases me—ran up and grabbed hold of me and punched me in the eye. Well, Raj told me, 'Ignore him, Curran, or you'll have worse trouble,' but I couldn't. I just got so mad. Because it wasn't fair. It wasn't fair that Nigel could beat me up like that when I was minding my own business. So I went for his nose. I never thought there'd be so much blood . . ."

The phone rang. "Christ," I said.

It was Jascha.

"I absolutely cannot talk right now," I said. "Give me half an hour."

I went back to Curran. "Who was that?" he asked.

"Jascha."

"Are you going to marry him?"

I laughed. "What a question!"

"Are you?"

"Goodness, no. We're working on the restrospective, that's all."

"But will you get married again, ever?"

I sighed. "Does the thought of that bother you?"

"A bit."

"Well, I can't give you a definite yes or no," I said, "but if I do find someone else, I think it'll be a long time from now. Okay?"

"Okay."

He flopped onto his back.

"Mum," he said, "are you mad at me?"

I folded my hands in my lap and stared down at them. I drew in my breath, and struggled to discern between several answers which spun through my head. No, that's what Riordan would have said. No, that's what Caroline would have said. Where were the words which were mine?

"No," I said. "I'm not mad at you. I think you had every right to be angry, because you're right. Life hasn't been fair lately. However, that doesn't give you an excuse to use Nigel Clark as a punching bag, even if he did hit you first. Promise me you won't get in trouble again?"

He closed his eyes, and nodded.

"That still looks pretty swollen," I said. "Stay here, and I'll get you some ice."

I went back to the kitchen and called Jascha. "What was it this time?" he asked. "Not another collision with the stockpot, I hope."

I told him about the incident at school.

"*Your* child did that? Tiny, quiet, unassuming Curran?"

"Yes."

"Wow."

"When I first heard what happened," I said, "I wanted to kill the little son of a bitch who gave him the black eye."

"But you can't fight his battles for him. You can't keep him cloistered."

"I know."

"What made him do it? Other than the fact that some eight-year-old psychopath jumped him, I mean."

"He said that he just got mad at the unfairness of things."

"Poor kid."

"He also asked me if I was going to marry you."

Jascha chuckled. "And your response?"

"No fucking way, sweetheart."

"Figuratively speaking."

"Of course. So, what did you want to talk to me about?"

"Galleries."

"Galleries?"

"Yeah, you know," he said, "little places to hang works of art in . . ."

"Cut it out. What about them?"

"Targeting ones that might be interested in Bill's work."

"And?"

"Like I said earlier, we're probably looking at the Hayward or Whitechapel. Tate's out of the question. Too big. Bill's not that established."

"Right," I said.

"What do you think?"

"Let's avoid the Hayward. Bill hated it. He called it a big concrete monster."

"And Whitechapel?"

"That's very ethnic, very young, sort of East End-y, isn't it?"

"Mmm-hmm. David Hockney had his first show there, I think."

"That sounds good," I said. "I've got to go. I promised Curran I'd bring him some ice."

I wrapped two pieces in a paper towel and carried them down the hall. When I stepped into his room, I found him curled up on his side, sobbing. I sat beside him. The ice numbed my shaky hands. A lump rose in my throat, and I swallowed it down. I set the paper towel on the nightstand and gathered him into my arms. "Go ahead and cry, love," I whispered. "You go right ahead." In the faded light of early evening we sat on the bed, and I held him, the same way that, with no questions, no obligations, I had been held, in Bill's arms.

Chapter Twelve

One January afternoon during my exchange year in London, I got
a phone call telling me that my father had gone into his study,
closed the door, pointed a gun at his head, and pulled the trigger.

I went back into the living room where I'd been taking notes
on the sofa, and with one swipe of my wrist knocked the books to
the floor. I knelt in the middle of the room and jammed my
knuckles in my mouth. In the bathroom, Pandora sang along with
a Kate Bush album as she shampooed the dye into her hair, and
Meg screeched, "Christ, would you turn down the bloody music?"

The doorbell rang. It was Bill. He picked his way around the strewn papers and got down beside me. He smelled of wool and fleece, aftershave and goodness. "Hey," he said softly. "Hey, love, you okay?"

I made a tiny noise deep in my throat. Wordlessly I pushed aside his shirt collar and put my cheek right next to his warm skin. On Pan's stereo Kate Bush wailed, *Do you know what I really need? Do you know what I really need?* and there on the floor he put his arms around me. We stayed like that for I don't know how long, barely breathing.

He took me back to his flat. We had peasant supper that night, soup and thick bread. He tore the crusts off his and swished them in the bottom of his bowl. As he scooped them into his mouth, broth clung to his chin. He looked like such a child that I wanted to laugh.

Instead I burst into tears. I sobbed so hard it hurt, it felt like I'd never be content in my own body again. He drew me around the side of the table and pulled me into his lap. I pressed my face against his neck. I wanted to dive beneath his skin. He kissed the edge of my mouth. I said, "Don't let go of me." We sat there in the kitchen until midnight, when he carried me into his bed.

Two days later, I woke. Morning sunlight hurt my eyes. I lifted my head from the pillow and glimpsed Bill by the door.

"You're getting up," he said.

I turned my face away from him and drew my knees to my

chest beneath the quilt. "No," I said. I slid my tongue over my cracked lips, moistening them.

"Yes," he said. He came into the room and stood beside me. With one hand he tossed the quilt back. I curled tighter. My teeth chattered. My calves spasmed with little shivers. I shook my head.

"Come on." He slung his arm around my shoulders and hoisted me up. I collapsed against him as he led me around the bed. Suddenly I felt conscious of the vinegary taste of too much sleep in my mouth and the grease in my hair. "You're going to take a shower," he said, voice steady, "and I'm going to make you breakfast, and then when you're awake we'll talk."

Grip tight, he guided me into the bathroom and turned on the shower. Its spray blasted me with cold droplets through the parted curtain. Tears filled my eyes. I gazed down, fingers numbly working up the buttons on my nightgown. He put his hands on my shoulders and kissed my forehead.

"You're going to have to trust me," he said, "when I tell you that sometime you're going to feel like living again. Can you trust me?"

I swallowed, and nodded.

"Okay," he said. "I'll be in the kitchen."

I stood trembling beneath the water for an hour, face in my hands. When I got out, I grabbed Bill's robe from a hook on the door and put it on. It was a faded cranberry color, imbued with his scent. I felt calmed as I padded into the kitchen. I sat down at the table and rested my head on my arms.

"It looks clean for once," I said.

"That's because everyone else is at class." Bill stood at the stove, making omelettes. He grinned. A bright-yellow nimbus glowed around his features. The room was so golden and gorgeous I felt as if I might break.

"What day is it?" I asked.

"Thursday."

"You have Advanced Life Drawing this morning, don't you?"

He nodded.

"Can you miss it?"

"I need to be here. That's all that matters."

"But—"

"Don't worry about it, love."

He brought a plate over, sat down across from me, and watched me eat. I hadn't realized how starved I'd been.

"Your mother called," he said.

"Oh, Jesus."

"She was lovely, very cordial, very businesslike. Not the virago I expected."

"That's her. Still Miss Manners in the face of grief."

I looked away. At the dishes in the sink, the sign penned in Bill's handwriting and taped above the counter: IF YOU GET IT OUT, PUT IT BACK. Below the order one of his roommates had scrawled SOD OFF, NEATFREAK!

"The funeral's tomorrow," he said.

"I know. I want to go, but—"

"It's all taken care of. Your mother wired money and I got a plane ticket. You leave at noon today."

"But my classes— The new term's just beginning—"

"I talked to Meg. She can straighten it out at university. She's bringing your things over, and I'll take you to the airport."

I sighed. "What would I do without you?"

"I should ask the same question," he said.

On the hour-and-a-half drive north from Baltimore later that night, I sat curled up in the front seat of my mother's car, sluggish with jet lag and newborn grief, head against the frigid windowpane. It wasn't until we passed the bright-blue sign grinning WELCOME TO PENNSYLVANIA that she finally spoke.

"I found him," she said.

She paused for a moment, then continued.

"He stayed home from work that day. Tuesday. Sure I thought it was odd, not like him at all, but I figured he'd just needed a break. You know how absolutely devoted to those scatterbrained kids he is. Was."

She turned a corner, and in the sudden glow of a streetlamp her features gleamed. Her slender, manicured hands gripped the steering wheel. Her wedding ring shone.

"I'd gone out on an errand in the morning. Had to pick up some theory books I'd ordered from the music store. When I got back, I was in a really good mood. I guess it was the snow glistening on the ground, the way your face and your fingers get all flushed when you come in from the cold. So I went and knocked on his study door to see if maybe he wanted to go downtown for lunch. But I got no answer."

I closed my eyes.

"There he was, on the floor. Flat on his back. His wrist splayed, the pistol beside him. Blood and brains everywhere. Like pain had melted his entire face."

"Don't say any more, Mom."

"I thought you'd want to hear this. I thought you'd need to know."

"Please. Just don't talk."

"After all, he's your father, and you two were so close, I can't see why you wouldn't—"

"Shut up!"

She clenched her jaw. In the darkness I glimpsed a spasm of nameless emotion—shock? pain? relief?—wrench its way across her face like a sharp ripple in silk. She turned again, onto our road, and I watched the elegant but ostentatious hodgepodge of houses—contemporary redwood, sprawling stone, precise neo-Colonial—slide by us. Through picture windows, bay windows, French doors, I caught sight of slender girls in fuzzy sweaters, doing their homework at expensive cherrywood tables in their brightly lit dining rooms, talking to their boyfriends in their warm custom kitchens, phone cords twined around their delicate fingers as they whispered banal love-words and lifted pale gorgeous eyes to monitor the snow's fall on their lawns.

"So is it good to be home?" my mother asked softly.

"No," I said.

We snaked up the driveway, and with the touch of a button beside her the garage door opened, its backward-scraping motion a sort of surreal magic to my exhausted eyes. After she parked the car she just sat there. The key still in the ignition. Her profile blank.

"Thanks . . . thanks for postponing things a day for me," I said. "I know it must've—must've been hard."

"Don't thank me. You had to be here."

She leaned down and rubbed her temples, features tight, then with a shuddering noise halfway between a sob and a sigh dropped her head in her hands. I thought of touching her shoulder, of the strangled cry in my own throat which, if released, might reach her, this sad, stricken other woman. But then she lifted her chin, my mother again.

"I'll have to get the rug cleaned," she said.

As we walked back to the car after the burial the next morning, all I could think about was taking off my nylons and ending the hurt and seeing Bill again. "Why did you wear those awful army boots?" my mother asked. "They look awkward with a dress, and given the occasion they're disrespectful."

"If you'd shown respect to a person who'd needed it years ago," I said, "there'd be no need to have this occasion."

She bit her lip and turned her face away. Pain cramped her laugh lines, those slight wrinkles which were misnomers since I had trouble recalling her laughter. In mourning colors she looked ashen. She should have been wearing cream and mulberry and rose. I should have been in my flat studying for an exam on Virginia Woolf, Bill's head in my lap.

But we weren't.

The minute we got back to the house, I tore upstairs and out of my clothes, ripped the pins from my hair, and collapsed on my bed. I screamed into the comforter so she wouldn't hear me, and then I put on jeans and a heather-blue sweater, things I knew she'd like, and went downstairs again. The outfit made her smile as I came into the kitchen.

"Mom," I said. "About what I said earlier. I didn't mean to insult you."

I couldn't explain to her how what she considered disrespectful in me was what my father had encouraged most. I didn't dare tell her that in a mean way, an honest way, a subtle way, what I had apologized for was the truth.

"Hey, I've made stupider statements in my life, believe me," she said. "It's okay."

She lit a fire in the den fireplace. I lay down in front of it, wanting to curl up and sob everything out of me until I was parched and new again, calmed by the flickering flames. I went over Woolf's dominant metaphors in my mind, analyzing them. I was on the angel whose heart gets shattered by an inkpot when Bill called.

My mother brought the phone to me; she thought I was asleep. She touched my shoulder. Her face was all glowing shadows. Its concern made me think I could love her, but part of me still cringed. I waited until after she left the room before I put the receiver to my ear.

"Hi," he said. "How are you doing?"

I closed my eyes. "Talk to me," I said, "just talk to me." He did. His voice was a narcotic, a protective membrane encircling me through the transatlantic wire. On my fingers I counted off the number of hours until I'd be in London.

He met me at Heathrow and took me to a Chinese restaurant in Bloomsbury, and we sat at a candlelit table adorned with wax roses. He quizzed me on *To the Lighthouse*. I kissed him and tasted the sweet-and-sour sauce on his lips. This is home, I thought. I'm never leaving here again.

After we ate, we walked up and down Gower Street in the slick, shining darkness. He laced his arm through mine. "I want to marry you," he said.

"I want to *be* you," I said.

"So I take it you agree?" he asked, laughing.

"Unequivocally," I said.

The next night I told the girls while we washed dishes. They shrieked and wrapped their arms around me.

"What, no ring yet?" Meg asked.

"Go easy on him, he's a starving artist," said Sarah.

"Next time, I'd marry for money, though."

"Shut up, Meg," I said. "There isn't going to be a next time."

"Have you picked a date?" Sarah asked. "Have you made any plans?"

"I've only been engaged for twenty-four hours," I said. "Give me a break. Although I definitely know I'll be recruiting you wild women as bridesmaids."

"I'm sure as hell not going to wear anything flouncy and pink!" This from Pan by the drying rack.

"Very funny," I said, and threw a dishtowel at her.

Eliciting a positive response from my mother wasn't as easy.

"You've known him two months and you want to marry him?" she asked.

"Yes."

"Don't you think that's rushing things?"

"For some people. Not for me."

"You sound like you're being impulsive."

"So were you."

On her end of the line there was silence.

"How long did you know Dad when you got engaged?"

"Three months."

"I rest my case."

"But, Gloria," she said, "that didn't—"

"Didn't what?"

"That didn't work out."

"Finally! Twenty-three years it takes her, but she speaks the truth at last!"

"Cut the theatrics," she said. "I don't want to argue with you."

"Neither do I."

"But are you sure about this?"

"Would I be doing it if I weren't?"

"I did."

"Mom. Stop. I love Bill."

"You may believe you do, but let me ask you this: do you love him, or are you just tempted?"

"Don't belittle what I feel."

"I'm not. I just know how it is. To be tempted. To be charmed by an accent and an earnest face and a vicious need."

"He's not another Riordan, damn it!"

"Did I say he was? All I'm asking you to do is make sure you know what you want to do and do it for the right reasons. Be careful."

"Mom, don't lecture me. You made the same decision I did when you were my age."

"Which is exactly why I'm lecturing you." She sighed. "Listen, I know you didn't call me to get my approval, but I just don't want you to make my mistakes."

"It's not a mistake. If you . . . if you could only meet him. Seriously. Come here, meet Bill, and you'll know."

"Is that an offer I'm hearing?"

"Yes. It is."

"Bill," she said. "Is he complicated?"

I knew exactly what she meant. Bill had his quirks, his paradoxes, his idiosyncratic range of emotions and secrets like anybody, but he wasn't that. *Complicated* meant capable of betrayal, full of bad hunger, facades, a man like a Chinese puzzle.

"No," I said.

"Thank God," she said. "I didn't mean to interrogate you. If you're happy, that's all that matters."

"If I put in a quarter, will you say that again?"

"Oh, Gloria. Please."

I laughed. "No, really, Mom. You're too classy for clichés. If I told you that I spent my teenage years as a murderess, chopping up men with pickaxes and burying them in the backyard, would you still say that as long as it made me happy, you approved?"

"Hell, no. I'd get you incarcerated. Now, your father, on the other hand—"

"Would have dug their graves for me," I said softly.

In June I flew back to the States to graduate, summa cum laude. Bill came with me, and we drove to New York City with my mother, who took us to the Russian Tea Room. She chattered and laughed and grabbed Bill's arm all through dinner, looking younger than I in her strappy heels and filmy pink dress. After a few glasses of champagne she launched into tales of my childhood, which Bill endured with a wry smile. "You know I'm incredibly proud of her," she said, "but it does surprise me that she's gone on for a degree in English. You should have seen her when she was six, Bill—curled up with a stack of her father's chemistry textbooks, amused for hours. It was adorable."

I kicked her under the table. She didn't flinch.

"I thought for sure she'd major in the sciences, the way she loved them then, the way she adored her father. They were quite . . ." She paused. "Quite kindred spirits."

"Gloria's told me," Bill said.

"I'm sure," she said. "But anyway, I should have expected. Gloria tends to surprise us. She's always been a bit of a rebel."

"A successful rebel," I said under my breath.

Bill heard me. "Well, it's a dead good thing," he said, laughing as he stroked the inside of my wrist, "because thanks to Nora Barnacle here and her final thesis, I now actually have a bloody clue as to the point of *Finnegans Wake*."

My mother beamed. When Bill got up to go to the bathroom, she leaned across the table before I could chastise her for her askew storytelling and whispered, "All my doubts are gone, Gloria. You've got fabulous taste."

"I never thought I'd hear that from you," I said.

"I must admit, I'm a bit jealous," she said. "He's an angel, absolutely sweet. Plus he's got great teeth—for an Englishman, that is."

I snorted. "Mom, you're awful."

"I try." She smiled, then leaned back in her chair and crossed her arms. She turned her head to gaze at Bill as he made his way towards our table. She blinked hard. Her lip trembled. She said, "He's what Riordan should have been."

On the flight home, Bill said, "Your mum is smashing. From what you told me, I was anticipating some middle-aged martyr with a monstrous ego."

I laughed. "You've got to understand that all the skeletons in my mother's closet are tightly zipped in garment bags," I said, and rested my head on his shoulder and slept until we landed.

And so we got married and had a baby and bought a nice little third-floor walkup in Islington before the area got fashionable, and thought we'd live happily ever after.

But it wasn't that simple. We forgot the Jim Jones/Santayana creed. Yes. The one about condemning the past and being doomed to repeat it.

Chapter Thirteen

Two months after Bill died, my mother called and told me she wanted to come to England.

"You've got to be kidding me," I said.

For years she'd tried to reach across the Atlantic Ocean to me through the contents of a box, an envelope: flowery, elegant cards on my birthday each July, expensive sweaters at Christmastime, cheery letters, presents for Curran. She'd flown to London but once since my permanent move there, and then only for the weekend of my wedding. All splashy florals and affectation, boyfriend on her arm, she waltzed from guest to guest in Bill's parents' Lamberhurst garden while silently I stood beside Bill, her careless kiss numb on my cheek, and swore I'd never let her set foot in the sanctuary of our flat on Theberton Street.

When Curran was born the following March, I begged Bill to be the one to call her from the hospital. "I'm exhausted," I said, running a hand through my tangled hair as I leaned down to smudge my lips across my newborn son's fragile forehead. "I can't deal with her right now."

"You weren't too knackered to talk to *my* mother," Bill said.

"I know, but please, just do this for me, all right? She likes you. She won't interrogate you."

"Okay, love," he said, shaking his head as he went out into the hall.

He came back ten minutes later. "How was it?" I asked.

"You make it sound like talking to her is torture."

"Sometimes it is."

"Well, it was fine. More than fine. She's so bleeding excited I had to tell her goodbye about five times before she'd hang up. She wants to come visit. When you've had time to rest, she said."

I yawned. "All right, I'll have to take about fifteen years, then."

"Crikey Moses, Gloria," he said, sitting beside me on the bed and taking Curran from me so I could comb out my hair in earnest, "why won't you meet her halfway?"

"I refuse to rearrange my life for someone who's so gushingly in denial."

"Suit yourself," he said, "but I still think you're being terribly ridiculous."

I flipped my hair upside down and worked out a particularly bad snarl, then lifted my head, leaned over, and drew him to me, two fingers beneath his chin. "You go through eight hours of labor and see if you aren't," I said, and kissed him, a hard *I'm-back-from-hell* kiss, deep and long. Just then, Curran twitched in sleep. I laughed and gathered him back into my arms, pressed my cheek to his warm scalp, and thought: *mine.*

When I carried him into our flat for the first time two days later, there were four messages on the answering machine. I listened to the first one—*"Gloria, I'm so happy for you, and I'd love to . . ."*—and then hit the ERASE button.

"You can be really cold sometimes," Bill said from the doorway.

"So can she," I said.

But she kept trying. Once a week, at first, then every two weeks. I left the machine on, or had Bill field her calls for me. "Tell her I'm in the shower," I said, toweling off my wet hair in the kitchen. "Tell her I'm hormonal and crazy because of Curran and I need a nap."

"You're still going to be using that excuse when he's twenty, aren't you?" he asked.

"Probably," I said, and skulked out of the room, arms wrapped around myself, feeling miserable.

One late December afternoon, after the calls had trickled

down to one every six weeks at best and I figured she'd given up, the phone rang. Bill got it. I kept my back to him, down on the floor in the living room with a then nine-month-old Curran. Bill came up behind me, put his hands on my shoulders. "Gloria," he said, "don't you think it's time you stopped this game?"

"What do you mean?"

"You know what I mean. Your own sodding mother is on the phone wanting to wish you a happy Christmas, and here you sit hiding out like she's your worst enemy."

"That's not a bad approximation."

"Look," he said, "I'm not going to referee this one anymore."

"All right," I said, and grabbed his arm to pull myself up off the carpet. Curran's eyes widened, inquisitive. "Back in a bit, darling."

"Yeah, Mom," I said, picking up the kitchen phone.

"Gloria," she said, voice high-pitched with a fusion of delight and hurt. "Sweetheart, almost a year of not talking to you, and this is all I get, 'Yeah, Mom'?"

"Motherhood chinks away at your ability to articulate. When you spend all day with someone who has a five-word vocabulary, you don't exactly quote Shakespeare anymore."

She laughed, but then turned clenched. "That's not what I meant, and you know it."

"Mom. Damn it. I don't have time for this."

"For me."

"No, I didn't say that . . . I mean, yes, I'm busy, I have a life over here, I have a child, I—"

"You have a mother."

"When she feels like being one."

"Gloria, for Christ's sake, I'm trying to—"

"Trying to what?"

"To start over."

"What a coincidence. So am I. Well, there we go, Mom, that's just perfect. You've got your new life with your smart little condo, your ever-so-hot lawyer, your first chair in the symphony, and I have mine with Bill and Curran. Now why can't we see this on the same wavelength? We move on, we respect boundaries, we make no strained attempts at warm fuzzies."

"Damn it, Gloria, can't you see that I never had a chance—"

I heard a loud thud, and Curran crying in the next room.

"Mom," I said, "I have to go. Curran needs me."

Her voice softened. "How is he?"

"He's gorgeous," I said.

"God, I'd love to see him."

"Well, who knows," I said sweetly, angry panic rising like steam inside me as Curran's wails battered my ears. "What with that lovely piece of meat you had draped all over you at my wedding, you could find yourself in my position pretty soon—you're still young enough, and, Jesus, how old could he have been, twenty-four, twenty-five? Or is he an artifact now?"

"Don't go there. Don't even think it. You live like I did, Ms. 'I Have Complete Control of My Life Now That I Married an Englishman,' you live one fucking year like I did, and you will never begrudge me the happiness I have right now again."

"Gloria?" Bill called from the living room.

"Mom," I said, swallowing hard, "I'm hanging up the phone in about five seconds, so if you want to get any messages of holiday cheer out of the way, you'd better do it now."

"Merry . . . Merry Christmas," she said softly.

I hung up and slammed my fist down hard on the kitchen counter, then went back in to Curran and Bill. They stared at me with bemused expressions from where they sat on the Oriental rug, Curran in Bill's lap.

"What happened in here?" I asked.

"His usual 'I'm-trying-so-bloody-hard-to-walk-but-I-can't' spills," Bill said, stroking back the damp blond strands of Curran's hair, which gleamed reddish-gold in the light from the Tiffany lamp behind him. "What happened in *there*?"

"Mudslinging, honey," I said. "Pure and simple."

"Did you clean up the kitchen?"

I smiled and sat down beside him. "Not yet."

He noticed my reddened knuckles, and touched the side of my face. "Gloria, you really ought to give her a chance."

I leaned up to kiss the top of his head. "You are the world's biggest peacemaker, and I love you for it," I said, "but you have just got to understand that my mother and I are destined to be at each other's throats forever."

"Yeah, well, do it quietly," he said. "You were scaring Curran."

I held out my arms to my son, and he beamed. "No more yelling," I said. "Mummy promises, okay?"

My own mother and I wouldn't hear the sounds of each other's voices again until after Bill was dead.

• • •

Now I drummed my fingers on the kitchen counter, hesitating before I spoke for fear that I'd burst out in either a laugh or a scream.

"You have *got* to be kidding me," I said again.

I could hear her on the other end of the line, sharply drawing in her breath.

"I just want to see you and Curran," she said.

"Please, not this game again."

"Gloria, I only thought that after Bill you might need . . ."

I'd sent her a brief letter, scratchy with shock, right after his death. I hated to do it, but she and Bill had liked each other, and I'd always felt a compulsion to let her know, at least perfunctorily, about the major events in our lives: my new job, Bill's work on an experimental show, Curran's excellent marks. I never expected her to respond with a request—or was it an offer?

She paused.

"You don't want me to come, do you?"

"Well, after all the shit we've been through over this one—"

"I know it won't be easy, and maybe I'm asking too much, but I'd just like to—"

"Jesus, Mom, don't do this to me! You really think I need this stress right now?"

"Only you would think of an honest conversation with your mother as hazardous to your mental health."

"Only you would believe that after countless brawls with you I could just banter away blithely and say, 'Sure, catch the next plane from Baltimore to London, no problem.' "

Her voice tightened. "We don't have to be this way, you know. We can work through this, we can make things better. Or at least try. That's all I want. A chance."

"Yeah, well, that's very noble, and if you put a gun to my head"—I winced at my own choice of words—"I'd have to agree with you, but you've got to understand something."

"Yes," she said, slightly breathy, waiting for the great confession, the blissful moment of closeness.

"I am an absolute fucking mess. I can barely scrape dinner together without losing my mind, much less patch up every splintery relationship in my life right now."

"I know."

Do you really? I wondered, rubbing a hand across my eyes.

"Mom, I'm tired," I said. "I can't play the flawless hostess."

"You don't have to. I can help you, honey, I'd be glad to, I mean, God, if you ever need someone to take over with Curran when he gets on your nerves, I'd love to volunteer, after all I haven't seen him—"

"You had to work that in there, didn't you?" I said. "Look, if you want to come visit us, then come visit us. I'd like to end this charade once and for all."

"Oh, I'm so glad. I can book a hotel somewhere if you want. I know there isn't exactly a dearth of them up where you are, but if it'll make things easier for you—"

"No," I said suddenly, surprising myself, "it's all right. You don't have to do that. You can stay here."

"Really? You're sure it won't be any trouble?"

Mountains of it, I thought. "I don't think so. Just don't expect the Savoy."

She laughed. "I'm performing in my concert series until April thirtieth, so I'm aiming for the first week in May, if that's all right."

I told her it was, hung up the phone, and returned in a what-have-I-done stupor to the table, where I'd been grading papers. The phone rang again. It was Jascha.

"Good news," he said. "I got Whitechapel."

"You're kidding."

"I'm not."

"For when?"

"May. We open the fifth."

I groaned.

"What's wrong? I thought that was terrific, considering how most places are booked into the next century."

"Oh, it is, but my mother's probably coming to London that week."

"What's the problem with that?"

"Just . . . everything."

"You sound like you could use a stiff drink."

"Hell, yes."

"I know the perfect place for one," he said. "I'll be over."

I sent Curran down to the Romdourls', and Jascha took me to a restaurant called Nikita's on Ifeld Road. We sat and sipped lemon vodka.

"Could I ask you something?" I asked.

"Sure."

"Why are you so damn nice to me? You buy me dinner, you sit and listen to me ramble, you kindly validate every word I say. Why do you take the time, other than because I'm the executor of Bill's estate? Do you want to sleep with me, or what?"

He laughed, then grew pensive.

"I take the time," he said, "because where you are is where I've been." He looked away. "So, what's the deal with your mother?"

"My mother," I said, "is fifty-three but looks forty. She's skinny and stylish and blond and a brilliant musician. She eats at French restaurants every night of the week and lives with a younger man."

"She sounds cool."

"Oh, she's very cool," I said. "Ripened by age. In control of her life for the first time. In bloom."

"So why disparage her?"

"Because she wants us to be pals. She'd love for us to trade recipes and clothes, to whisper conspiratorially and grab each other's hands when we're excited, to have deep conversations about the mysterious bonds of blood and bone one moment and bitch about how long it takes to clean the bathroom the next."

"And that can't happen?"

"No, it can't happen. I can't be her best friend right now, because she wasn't my mother when I needed her to be."

His eyebrows furrowed.

"You're confused, aren't you?" He nodded. "Well, then, I think it's time for a little story."

We paid the bill for the drinks and went outside. "Let me give you the abridged version," I said. "When my father was at Oxford, he was engaged to a beautiful genius. She died. My mother came over on a Fulbright. She was angry and frustrated; he needed a pair of strong arms around him. They got married, went back to the States, and guess who was born of their misguided passions? My mother became a bitch. My father became a parasite. Night after night I listened to him weep, blotted the tears from his swollen eyes, and she let me carry the burden. When I was twenty-one, I came to London. Three months later, my father put a bullet in his brain, and her marvelous life took off from there."

"Aren't you oversimplifying things?"

"Of course I am. Of course I know it wasn't all her fault, and in a way I feel sorry for her. Her parents wanted her to marry a morally upstanding young man; she only wanted to make love to a cello. Do I blame her for pulling away from him, for being angry? No. Do I fume when I think of how she left me unprotected, the victim of a sort of emotional incest? Yes."

We walked along in silence for a while. The effort to verbalize that which felt wordless, to clarify the ambiguous, sent a tiredness through my veins.

"There's a story by Joseph Conrad," I said, "in which a young man of one tribe loves a girl from another. He and his brother hatch a plan for the two of them to sail away and elope, and as they're about to push the boat from the shore, these angry tribesmen, out for blood, approach him, and the boy has to make a decision: to stay and save his brother, keeping his loyalty intact, or to climb into the boat where the girl he loves waits."

"And who does he choose?"

"The girl."

Jascha chewed his lip in silent meditation.

"I did it without a thought," I said. "Shoved off from the shore, gave up my allegiance to my home, my parents. With Bill, I rowed towards the sun. I honestly believed that I'd find 'a country where death would be forgotten.' "

He put his hand on my arm. "You look cold," he said. "My flat's just down the street. Do you want to go in for a bit?"

In his living room's cluster of black leather couches and sling chairs, amongst pyramid-shaped lamps and metal sculptures, I sat next to Jascha, hands folded in my lap, head down so I wouldn't look at his face and shatter.

"It's funny," I said, "but I finally understand what my parents did, because I'm doing it."

"How do you mean?"

"Well, one time when I was about nine, I guess, I asked my father why he married my mother if he didn't love her as much as he had his fiancée who'd died, Adrienne, and he said, 'She was a warm body. She was there. I needed to forget.' At the time I thought that was a mean, callous thing to say, but now—shit, now I know what he meant, and why, because I feel his need, the irrationality of it. I wake up every morning to a half-empty bed. And you know what's awful? You know what's so terrible, what right now I'm thinking?"

"No."

I laughed. I laughed, and trembled. "Right now," I said, "I'm sitting here and thinking, I'm thinking that I want to kiss you, I want to kiss you just so I can remember how it felt, and, Christ, what am I saying? You aren't Bill. You aren't Bill."

My hands flailed in inept gestures. My lips curled back in a sob as tears slid down my cheeks.

"I've got to stop crying," I whispered. "I've got to stop, but . . . Why, damn it? Why not a drug dealer, why not me . . . and him? I would've given him my marrow. I would've gladly killed anybody."

He moved closer, reached out his hand.

"Don't touch me," I said. "Please don't touch me, because if you touch me, I'll explode, I'll detonate, I'll turn to you, I'll be dangerous, I'll do something desperate, and, oh, God, Jascha, I know why they did it, I know how it feels to hurt so bad you want to hurt somebody, and where do I go from here? Jascha, I'm scared. . . ."

He put his arm around me and drew my cheek against his shoulder. "I'm sorry," I said. I stared up at his face and thought how easy it could be—lift my chin, reach out my fingers, press my quavery mouth to Jascha's, find oblivion, beg him to save me.

"Don't be," he said.

"When we were at Nikita's," I said, "you told me that the reason you take time to listen to me is because you've been where I am. What—"

"About four years ago," he said, "my wife and five-year-old daughter were killed in a car accident."

I closed my eyes. Thought of the Shelley poem I'd used with my fourth-form students as an example of meter gone awry. Death is here, and there, and everywhere.

"I used to watch you," he said, "on the nights when you met

Bill at the studio. You'd have on a long black dress and a big baggy coat, and your hair would be gathered up except for one little curl that escaped right here"—he touched my jaw—"and you'd have Curran with you. Bill would drop what he was doing and run over, excited as a child at the sight of the two of you, and he'd put his arm around your waist and you'd all walk out for fish and chips, and as much as I respected him as an artist, God, how I hated him then, for what he had, that gorgeous, happy triangle, that glistening, flaunted safety . . ."

He laughed. It was my dangerous laugh. Help-me-I'm-falling.

"I hate to admit this," he said, "but you occupied my thoughts a lot then. I felt silly—I mean, I hadn't said a word to you, and didn't even know your name. You were just Bill's American wife. Still, I looked for pieces of Marianne in you, and found them: the way you kept your head down with a wry smile on your lips, the motions of your hands when you spoke. Why do we do it, Gloria?"

"I don't know."

"I still try," he said. "And it's been years. All those TV-movie-type-things you say you do? I do them, too. I see a little dark-haired girl wearing a pink ruffled dress in Hyde Park, and I whirl, the syllables of her name slide from my throat. 'Elizabeth,' I cry, and the poor thing's eyes widen. 'Mummy, why'd that man call me that? Doesn't he know my name's Anna?'

"And toy stores, oh, Jesus, don't even let me get near one. I walk past Hamleys, and I hear her saying, 'I want this, Daddy, and this, and this,' and I think, it's her birthday soon, she'll be nine, or should be, and it won't be long before she turns to boys in leather jackets who run their fingers down her spine, and like a fist uncurling, she'll ripen. . . ."

"Despite what people say, it doesn't get any easier, does it?"

"After a while there's a sort of dulling, a dulling that has to happen if you're ever going to get out of bed in the morning and do laundry and make breakfast without bursting into tears. I used to read newspaper stories of kids who'd fallen into frozen ponds and stayed submerged for half an hour, forty-five minutes, an entire hour, and lived. 'How do they do it?' I wondered then, but now I know, because grief isn't much different than their survival. After you reach a certain point of unbearable cold, there's a mechanism of shutdown. Blood slows. The organs and passions go sluggish. You do what you have to, and you do it well."

"Necessary madness," I murmured.

"Right, and then all of a sudden you'll settle into a comfortable chair to read, and the sun will slant across the page. You'll swell with joy, you'll think you've never before seen a thing of such beauty, and then you'll remember: I did, I *did*.

"So, in answer to your question, no. The pain becomes more subtle, but there's nothing easy about this."

"When Bill was at his sickest," I said, "and the possibility of his dying was at its strongest, I told myself I was lucky. Better for it to happen slowly, I reasoned. Better to know, to have time to prepare myself, to prepare Curran for the fact that in a matter of weeks or months he wouldn't have a father. Stupid of me, wasn't it? Because there's no 'better' way to die. Death isn't qualifiable."

I lifted my head from his shoulder and fumbled through my

purse. "I need a cigarette," I said. He smiled as I leaned back, lit one, and inhaled.

"When you told me about the Conrad story," he said, "it reminded me of the questions I face. Questions of loyalty, of the ethics of rowing away, so to speak. What do you do when your Siamese twin stops drawing breath? Do you carry the dead body fused with yours, drag it the rest of your life, or do you plant your feet firmly in the earth?" He sighed. "My wife and my daughter are phantoms, and I don't know whether I should hold on to them or reach for something tangible."

"That's what I'm afraid of," I said.

"I know," he said. "Hell, when you were being your usual cynical self at Nikita's and asked me if I wanted to sleep with you, I almost said yes."

"You didn't."

"I did. And then I thought, 'Just because she's attractive and going through the same agony you are, that's no reason to throw yourself at her. One good fuck won't magically make your lives better."

"No," I said, "it won't."

I checked my watch.

"It's getting late," I said, and stood. He walked me to the door and handed me my coat. I shrugged into it and pulled on my gloves. "Thank you for the drink," I said. I took his face in my leather-clad hands and kissed his forehead.

"What was that for?" he asked.

"For being there," I said. "For giving me hell's highway map."

I turned to leave, and he caught my arm.

"Gloria," he said. "That story about the couple in the boat. You never told me the ending."

"They have a few years of bliss," I said, "but then the woman dies with a raging fever and the man is forced to contemplate his choice."

"They never find a country where death can be forgotten."

"No," I said. "There is no such place."

Chapter Fourteen

When Bill suddenly grew pale and tired, we brushed off his symptoms, attributed them to working too hard. It wasn't until he joked about having a map of the world in bruises on himself that I insisted he see a doctor, and even then I wasn't overly concerned. At the worst, I expected him to come home with a bottle of iron pills and orders to eat more leafy vegetables.

The day of his appointment was gorgeous, a harbinger of spring, the colors of the sun and sky so crisp it hurt to look out the window at them. Curran was downstairs with Raj, so I had the flat to myself as I did the breakfast dishes. While I dried them, I was struck with a rare, delicious flash of euphoria, of cohesion: I'm thirty years old, I've got a wonderful, gentle artist for a husband and an adorable, bright little son, and I'm perfectly all right with myself. This is incredible. This is my life.

Then I heard Bill's key in the lock and the sound of his tossing his jacket over the back of the living-room couch. He came into the kitchen, walked up behind me, wrapped his arms around my waist, and rested his cheek against my neck. I sensed a solemnity, a sadness in the way he held me, and so I stared at the jars full of herbs perched on the sink-ledge to steady myself: a focal point, like in labor. "Gloria," he said. "I need to talk to you."

He sat me down at the table. He leaned forward, elbows on the Formica. His pale gray eyes gazed into my face as if he were fighting for solid ground, fighting not to shatter. He opened his mouth to speak. I wanted to reach across and brush my detergent-soaked fingers over his lips, stop the words from flying out. He said, "He thinks it might be cancer."

Eclipse. My vision swung out of focus. Blood surged through my ears with a roar. I skimmed my hands over the tabletop and braced myself for the terrible fall, but it never came. The sun and the sky and the breakfast dishes and the herb jars were still there, and my husband still sat before me in his plaid flannel shirt, holding my wrists, telling me not to worry as he rambled on and on about medical advances and bone-marrow biopsies and not jumping to conclusions just yet. Then Curran burst back in, blond and breathless, babbling about the new game Raj just got, and we had to smile, we had to nod, we had to pretend. We

forced our voices into the high, cheerful register of parents bent
on deception.

That night I tricked myself into believing that I would crawl
into the cocoon of sleep and wake up the next morning to find
Bill whole and smooth and unblemished, with no traces of the
day before in sight.

Instead I woke to a brightness that drove my eyes closed
again, and the truth so heavy it was like a pair of giant hands
pinning me to the mattress. I stared at Bill's shoulder blades and
willed myself not to cry.

After a while I propped up on one elbow and leaned over to
look at his face. He slept with his mouth slightly parted, breath
light as a child's, body slack with pleasure and unconscious aban-
don. I marveled at the wild asymmetry of his too-broad features,
his passion-roughened brown hair, the pale curve of his neck and
the throbbing vein that ran down it, as yet unscarred, a blue
river. How, I wondered, could someone so perfect possibly have
such vileness blooming inside him?

When he woke, he turned over, rested his hand against my
cheek, and pulled me closer so that our foreheads touched on the
pillow. We stared into each other's eyes, not with the languid
drowsiness of love, but with full knowledge of the grave turn our
lives had just taken.

On the first day of spring, a man sheathed in white shoved a
needle into Bill's hip and drew out a syringeful of his marrow. I
had a fourth-form class at the time, and was trying to explain

T. S. Eliot's concept of the objective correlative to a group of uninterested fifteen-year-olds, but I couldn't stop thinking about the long, thick metal piercing flesh.

I called home after lunch.

Bill answered. I'd begged him to let me pick him up at the hospital, but he'd insisted he could get home on his own. "Hi, love," he said. His voice sounded thin.

"How are you?"

"Fine. A little sore."

"How was it?"

"Your usual garden-variety agony."

"Bill, please. How was it really?"

"Painful. Dead painful. Long."

"Do you know when we'll get the results?"

"Day after tomorrow, probably."

"Will you be all right until I get home?"

"I'll be fine."

"You're sure? Because if you want me to, I'll leave early. It won't be a problem."

"Don't worry about me."

"I can't help it."

"I know, but try not to, okay? Whatever happens, happens."

Sometimes I thought we were locked in our roles, handcuffed to certain attributes: Bill the protector, Bill the optimist, Bill the rock, the endomorph, all flesh, and me the protected, off-kilter, fatalistic one, all bones and angles.

"Gloria? Are you still there?"

"Yes, but I'd better go. I've got a class in five minutes."

"I love you," he said.

"I love you, too." The parroting, the reverberation, one sentence, tiny, compact, driving the voice into a higher pitch, curving the lips back in primeval cry—*I love you; you must live!*—and splintering me, splintering me, oh, don't hang up, please not that click, that finality.

I drifted through the third-form class, the sixth-form class, instructions and assignments and criticisms tumbling from my mouth, my gaze fixed not on my students but on some far-off plane, all my energy cathected upon one glowing objective: must get home to Bill, must get home to Bill.

I found him propped up on pillows on our bed, reading a book on Edvard Munch. He grinned, and patted the edge of the mattress. I slipped out of my heels and sat beside him. He held out his arms. I leaned into them, breathed him in like oxygen, inhaling the scent of his skin: warm, earthen, but with a foreign undertone of antiseptic, of crackly examining-table paper. He stroked my hair and rested his chin on the top of my head. "My angel," he said. We stayed there like that for a while, in the soft glow of the lamplight. A gentle rain drummed on the windowpane, and I thought, *Whatever happens, happens.*

Later I made tea, and we sat cross-legged on the quilt and drank it, passing the same cup back and forth. We talked about the Munch book, about the shy, nail-biting girl in my fifth-form class who was a published poet—anything to keep our minds off the phone call which would jangle us from our contentment, knock the walls down, signal the end of the world.

It came two nights later. I sat at the kitchen table, helping

Curran fix mistakes in his school composition. When the phone rang, it felt as if a firecracker had exploded inside my chest and was now burning its way through my body, but I stayed calm, stayed still and poised with my pen while Bill answered. "Look at this one, here, darling, it isn't so hard to change. You have down 't-h-e-r-e house,' but which word do you need?"

"The other one. T-h-e-i-r."

"Brilliant. Okay. Let's check the next sentence."

As I scanned, I listened to Bill. "Yes," he said. "Yes."

I pulled my chair closer to Curran's and put my arm around him. "The rest of this looks great. Better than a lot of the papers I get."

He giggled. "Really?"

"Really," I said, my lips against the curve of his ear.

"How soon?" Bill asked. I looked up. "Yes, of course, I understand."

He hung up the phone. Bit his lip.

"Curran," I said, "why don't you take your paper and get ready for bed? Could you do that for me?" He nodded and headed down the hall with a perceptive sort of obedience which I saw often in him and found frightening.

Bill and I stared at each other.

In those few seconds, I felt my skin peel away, felt every layer of me reduce to reddish-black blood and glistening bone. My whole body contracted. In my husband's face I saw the shock, the numbness, the truth.

And then I was falling, hurtling through empty space and into the black. Of all possible nightmares, that one is the worst. If you dream you're falling and you don't wake up, then you die. But I was already awake.

We had it all laid out for us. Like a medical Tarot.

The next night we went to the oncologist's office and sat amongst his obligatory ocean of books and papers and the smell of leather and despair. I stared at the diplomas on the walls. Bill put his hand over mine. Dr. Levitch, our card reader, twisted the cap on his fountain pen and told us about risks, reasons to be glad, dangers.

Bill's body was in a state of revolt. Like a rebellious teenager drunk on the taste of power, one immature myeloblast had gone on a rampage. The only way to destroy it, and its army of warped copies, would be to pump his veins full of toxic chemicals. They would nauseate him, ulcerate him, make him lose his hair. Fire with fire. Either way, Bill would get scorched.

The first round of treatment was set to begin the next day. There was no time to waste. The meter was ticking. Ten days in hell, a brief respite, then back again, and again, and soon it would be summer, all locusts and lushness. Three shots at the white corpuscle legion, and then we'd wait. And hope for a remission.

"Survival rates are good, but there are no guarantees," said Levitch. "A relapse is always possible. Shutdown of other organs, overwhelming infection . . ."

Of course there are no guarantees, I thought as I leaned back in my chair. *There are never guarantees with anything.* When Bill drew me into his arms that first time in the studio kitchen, I didn't know whether he would heal me or crush me, but there he sat, with me still, listening to the tale of what lay ahead.

It was almost seven by the time we took the tube home. On impulse we stopped at a chip shop on Upper Street. We sat at a table by the window and ate the haddock straight from the paper. Bill, for once, was silent. I watched him, my love with his grease-stained fingers and worn coat, and my anger boiled. I wanted to reach across the table and into his blood so I could kill every poisoned cell inside him.

We took a long time to eat, trying to preserve the grimy simplicity of the moment. Bill put his arm around me as we walked up our street in the darkness. We saw a light on in our son's window. I trembled to think of him pulling on his pajamas in an empty room, watching the clock with a child's unbearably slow perception of time. Bill's grip on me tightened. "What do I tell him?" he whispered in my ear as we came up the front steps.

"The truth," I said.

And so, fingertips touching, we sat on Curran's bed, one on either side, and in the gentle blue-tinged light explained the cruelties of the body to him. He lay beneath the sheets and gazed at us. "Dad will get better, though," he said. "Won't he?"

I opened my mouth. Bill spoke before I did.

"I can't make that kind of promise," he said, "but I will try my hardest to stay here with you."

At that point I went out in the hall and wept.

Later I sat on our bed and watched him undress, thinking, *This is the last time I will see this body unscathed, unbrutalized, free of pain.*

"It's not a death sentence," he said, folding his jeans and hanging them over a chair.

"No."

He sat down beside me. I turned one of his hands over and ran my finger across his palm. Across the lifeline.

"It's not like the flipping 1940s," he said, "when you were just taken home to die and had no hope." He swallowed, repeated himself as if doing so would convince either him or me or both of us. "It's not like that."

"Of course not," I said.

In a few hours, I thought, *he will be weak and broken and sucked dry in a sterile white bed, head spinning.*

He winced as accidentally I stroked a spledge of purple on his skin, a nascent bruise. An unnamed country.

"Bulgaria," he said, and grinned.

"Bill," I said, "what are we going to do?"

He flopped onto his back. "We're going to live," he said. "Now come here. I've got ten nights without you ahead of me."

And so I rolled over, into his waiting embrace, and when his hands reached beneath the thin fabric of my nightgown, I whispered *I love you, I love you* into his hairline, as if love were enough, as if love were armor, as if love were an amulet which could plunge us into light and out of darkness.

Chapter Fifteen

My mother met me at Heathrow with good intentions and too many suitcases, throwing her arms around me as if thirty years of our lives never happened. She babbled as we headed towards customs. "God, I can't wait to see how the city's changed, and *you*, just look at you, you're lovely—not that I ever expected you not to be, but you had to get out of that punk phase, that's all. . . ."

I didn't look at her. If I looked at her, there would be bloodshed or tears, so I nodded at her every word—yes, Mom, of course—and kept my gaze on the sign we were approaching, the one which read NOTHING TO DECLARE.

We took a taxi home. She grew solemn. There were no more brittle jokes like the one she'd whispered in my ear about hiding her Uzi before the airport security check. She was a graver version of my mother, that woman who sat beside me in a pink wool suit and pumps, legs crossed, blond curls stiff with perfection. She leaned against the door, body curled as if wounded, face turned towards the window. She had a run in her stocking. I thought I'd scream for joy.

While I lugged her bags inside, she ran about the flat, investigating my decor. "These are beautiful," she said as she fingered a pair of mosaic votives on the living-room table.

"Camden Passage," I said. "Five pounds. Get yourself some."

"And your kitchen!" she said, gesturing towards its wallpaper border of *trompe l'oeil* plums. "It's cozy, it's precious, it's—"

"Dirty," I said, and with a sigh set down her last suitcase. It was so like her to rhapsodize over things that didn't matter. "God, Mom, you're only staying a week. You didn't have to bring your entire wardrobe."

"I know, but I like to be prepared." She snorted and held up a jar which read ASHES OF DEAD LOVERS. "Where in the hell did you get this?"

"From the girls in my old flat. As a gag gift at my bridal shower."

"And you kept it?"

"Out of sheer sentimentality. It's in terrible taste, though, especially given our family history, don't you think?"

She looked away. "Maybe I'd better go unpack my things."

Sprawled on my bed, I watched her sort her clothes. Hanger by hanger her mauves and powder blues and beiges encroached upon the blacks and dark greens in my closet. She said, "I hate to kick you out of your room."

"I don't mind." The couch would be tight and soft, like an embrace. I'd volunteered to take it so I wouldn't have to face the taut expanse of sheet on Bill's side of the mattress.

My mother hung her last blouse and lined her shoes up in a row. She sat beside me, a little smile on her face. She patted my knee. She smelled like guilt and floral perfume. "I think we really needed this," she said.

Jascha called me two days later.

"Day after tomorrow," he said. "You ready?"

"I think so, but I can't say I feel any sort of thrill. It's going to be hard."

"I know."

Since our conversation that night in his flat, those two words had taken on a whole new power. They were no longer silence-fillers, no longer patronizing.

"How's life with Mommy dearest?" he asked.

I laughed. "No catfights yet. We're very civil, considering our history of screaming matches. I feel as if soon there'll be a shift, a fracture, something will happen, the masks will drop off our faces, and we'll either collapse in each other's arms or kill each other."

"If you plan on the latter, please do me a favor and wait until after May fifth."

"I'll try. And Jascha, she took us to Le Gavroche. Fucking Le Gavroche. Do you know how much that costs?"

"More than anyone should have to pay?"

"Exactly. I don't even like French food, and poor Curran, he thinks macaroni and cheese is a big deal, so he was awestruck, scared, really. Later he said to me, 'I know it'd hurt Gran's feelings if she heard this since she spent so much money, but I didn't like it there. There were too many different forks and I was afraid I'd spill something.'"

"How's he dealing with all this?"

"Oh, he thinks Caroline's neat. A real switch from Bill's mother. The other day he told her, 'I think you look younger than Mum,' so now she adores him. They look eerily alike."

"Are they coming to the retrospective?"

"I don't know. I mean, I hate to bar my mother from the thing, but . . ."

"She can come. I don't mind. I'll behave myself around her."

"I'm more worried about Curran."

"He wants to see it?"

"He's obsessed with it. I hate to tell him he can't go, but then again I have to consider what might happen if he did. The paintings, they're . . . what if he saw *Necessary Madness* and thought . . ."

"I can't decide for you, Gloria."

"No."

"But listen, I was thinking . . . about the opening . . ."

"Yeah?"

"You might not like this, but I thought maybe it would be a good idea if you wrote a brief bit, you know, something to read for that night."

"Oh, for God's sake. You want me to play the tragic widow? Give a eulogy? No."

"Come on."

"I'll be on display. I'll feel stupid. I'll be there rambling and making an inarticulate fool of myself and of Bill."

"You can articulate his work and his life better than anyone else."

"I guess so, but—"

"Please. Just a few words."

"Jesus, Jascha . . . I don't know. . . . I mean, if you really want me to, I can, but don't expect a tearjerker or a master's thesis, okay?"

"Thanks. I'm sorry to stick you with this so late."

"It's all right."

"Oh, and good luck with your mother."

She came in as I hung up the phone. "Who was that?" she asked.

"The person who's working on the retrospective with me."

"The sculptor?"

"How did you know?"

"Curran told me. 'He's dead good,' he said. 'He took us out to eat the night Mum tipped the pot off the stove and got a bit mental.' "

"Yeah. He did."

"Are you going out with him?"

"Jascha? Hell, no."

"You sound a little too vehement for me to believe you."

"Would it have bugged you if I'd said I was?"

"No, it's just that with Curran—"

"Oh, okay. Now you fight valiantly for the welfare of the child. Now you waver, you worry."

"Gloria, please. I was only trying to make the point that so soon it might put Curran in an awkward position. That you should think of him."

"You think I don't?" I said. "You think that twenty-four hours a day, every word I say and every move I make doesn't undergo scrutiny, isn't subjected to the question of 'How will this affect Curran?' You're a fine one to talk, seeing as five months after Dad died you were waltzing back out on the rebound."

"That isn't fair," she said. "You were older. You were living your own life."

"But it still bothered me."

"The situation was different. I had a right to do that."

"So what you're telling me is that because your marriage was awful, you were justified in fluttering on to someone else, but since mine was good I should pull out the black veil and bear my grief alone the rest of my days."

"Stop it. I don't want to argue with you. That's not what I came here for."

"If I hear you say that one more time," I said, "I'll scream. I don't want to argue with you, either, but I've lived with you long enough to know that doing it's the only way to find my mother inside this polished acquaintance who's standing before me. And I'm sorry if I have to be raw, and I'm sorry if I ruin the ambience of your London vacation, but the reason why I was so vehement about not seeing Jascha was because I am so fucking scared that I will before I'm ready. Are you satisfied now?"

She turned her back to me, but I could tell she was wiping her eyes. "I never did any dances on Riordan's grave," she said.

I took off work the next day. It pained me to think of her wandering the city alone, even though she'd insisted she still remembered its layout, and I felt bad about having made her cry.

"Do you need a dress for this exhibit?" she asked that morning at breakfast.

"No, Mom, I don't need a dress. I've got a black velvet one I bought a few years ago."

"Velvet? In May? Oh, honey, you really need to give up that black fetish. Let me buy you something different."

I sighed. "I take it you want to go shopping."

"Gloria," she said, "is the world round? Of course I want to go shopping."

We went to Harvey Nichols, and she bought me a long, cranberry-colored dress, simple but dramatic. "Okay," I said, "you put me through the classy Caroline Merchant routine. It's my turn."

"Uh-oh. Where are you taking me?"

I smiled. "To a place with studs and leather."

She gasped as I led her inside a store that looked more like a warehouse. "London Calling" blasted over a stereo system, and she laughed at me as I mouthed the words and steered her from rack to rack. She looked relieved when I grabbed a black pleated skirt, but then her eyes widened when on top of it I piled a black lace top, a white T-shirt snipped to rags, and a leather vest. "No more," she said.

"Just wait, this'll be fun," I said. "Accessories next."

I picked up fishnet stockings, a pair of Doc Martens, and a studded choker, then got a pink-haired girl to open a fitting room. I leaned against the wall and listened to my mother fumble and swear inside it.

"Gloria, these boots are killing me," she said. "How could you stand them?"

"Revolution wasn't supposed to be comfortable."

There was a brief pause, and then she said, "Oh, Jesus."

"Let me see."

"There's no way I'm coming out in this."

"Come on. You've seen me drunk; I can see you in leather. Open the door."

She stepped from the cubicle. We burst out laughing at the same time. Doubled over, we hobbled to the larger triptych of mirrors.

"I wish I had a camera," I said.

"Look at us," she said. "We've reversed."

I gazed at our reflections: my mother in rags with her boots half-laced, me in my long skirt and silk blouse, minimalist but tasteful in comparison.

"You're right," I said, "but for the full effect we'd have to give you spiked hair and a nose ring."

"Could you imagine? Think of me at a symphony concert in this. Of course a short skirt of any kind with a cello is pushing it."

"Do you want me to buy you the choker?" I asked. "You've spent so much on me, I owe it to you."

"Sure," she said. "It'll be a little souvenir to show David."

We grew quiet then. David was her thirty-year-old lawyer.

As we walked out into the street, she said, "You've never seen the place where your father and I lived, have you?"

"I've been to Earl's Court, yeah. Bill used to live there."

"I meant the actual flat."

"Oh, that, no."

"Would you like to?"

I nodded.

We took the tube there and walked past scores of fast-food restaurants. My mother's face fell. "It's so . . . touristy," she said.

"It's thirty years later," I said.

"There," she said suddenly, and pointed her finger across the street. "See it? On the second floor?"

"Yes."

It looks so ordinary, I thought. Gingham curtains. Shapes, the silhouettes of people's bodies inside, moving from couch to kitchen table to bed and then back again, unaware that in those rooms my parents had experienced their brief flicker of happiness.

"There was cabbage-rose wallpaper in the bedroom," she

said. "I'd wake up to that, and his head against my shoulder . . .
I wonder if it's still there. Maybe I should ring the bell, ask if I
could have a look around."

"No," I said.

She turned. "And over here," she said, "was where we'd
sometimes walk to a little diner for breakfast."

"Looks like it's a gay bar."

"No kidding."

We walked back towards the tube station.

"Did you love him?" I asked.

"Yes," she said. "No matter what you might like to think, no
matter how cold and unfeeling he may have made me out to be,
yes, I did."

"But all those years . . ."

"I know. We were separate, we were together alone. But
you've got to understand that your father—"

"Wanted you to be someone you weren't."

"Exactly."

"But you could have listened to him. You could have been
there."

"I could have, you're right. After a point, though, when the
flattery turned cloying, and his rich murmur of 'I want to exist for
you' faded to a desperate bleat of 'I want you to exist for me,' it
got hard."

"That's a pitiful excuse, Mom. That's selfish."

She nodded. "I realize that love requires a certain selflessness,
but your father asked for the wrong kind. What have you got if
you're loved for what you offer and not who you are?"

"Grounds for divorce."

She laughed. "Good girl."

"Then why did you stay with him?" I asked.

"He was safe," she said. "In his own quiet, warped way he idolized me. And there's enormous, seductive safety in idolatry."

"The thing that I don't understand," I said, "is why he had to be like that. What makes some people recover from grief with boundaries, with strength, while others falter? I mean, much as I yelled at you yesterday, I have to admit that I admire how you've gotten on with your life. What made you able to do it, and not him?"

"I don't know," she said.

I thought of my father and Adrienne, and the whole affair—the brilliant, pretty girl killed in a car crash before she could marry her fiancé, the shy, sensitive young man crushed by his loss—seemed too hokey to be real. But it had been. There had been that photograph with the quote from "Two in the Campagna."

"Have you got enough money for the tube fare?" my mother asked.

"More than enough," I said.

When we got home we dumped all our bags on the couch and sat on the rug to cut the price tags off what we'd bought. "Where do you want to go for dinner tonight?" my mother asked.

"Nowhere," I said, poised with the scissors. "You and Jascha

Kremsky have got me so spoiled I'm forgetting how to cook. I need practice."

"Do you mind if I turn on the radio?"

"Go ahead."

She knelt by the stereo and fiddled with the dial.

"Remember the contests we used to have," she said, "to see who could guess the composer first?"

"Yeah."

Music swelled from the speakers. She turned her head in my direction, daring me to get it right.

"Debussy," I said, and lit a cigarette.

That night, when she and Curran had gone to bed, I sat at the kitchen table with a blank sheet of paper in front of me, and tried to write the speech Jascha had asked for. After half an hour, all I'd done was scribble a childish proclamation of maiden initials and futility: *G.M. loves B.B.*

So what? I thought. Love wasn't a cure. Love couldn't outwit death.

Soon my English-teacher instincts kicked in, and I began to scribble full sentences. At one a.m. my mother came out in her nightgown.

"Did the light keep you awake? I'm sorry."

She sat beside me. "It's late," she said. "You've got circles under your eyes. You should get to bed."

"I have to finish this. It's for the retrospective."

She tucked a strand of hair behind my ear. I thought of her

firm hands on my shoulders, leading me back to my room after the nightmares when I was six, pulling me to her on the floor of my father's study when I was bloody-chinned and sixteen.

"Sweetheart," she said, "your fingernails."

"What about them?"

"They're bitten down. They're awful."

I looked up from my page and was about to remark that the state of my manicure was the least of my worries, but I stopped. Finally I understood her language. The talk of tube fares, dresses, gnawed nails—all wails of warning to a dark daughter, oh, you're slipping and I can't catch you, no matter how hard I try, no matter how sweet my grasp.

Chapter Sixteen

Most of the spring, Bill had lain in a hospital room with the shades drawn. In the evenings I sat beside him and graded stacks of students' exams while he slept. I'd be halfway through a kid's complaint that "Araby" wasn't a "real" story when he'd moan, and I'd scrape my chair over closer to the bed and hold his now-bare skull over a blue basin while he retched.

Afterwards, gasping, he lay back on the pillow, and I sponged his bile-stained mouth and hot face. He gazed first at me, then at the tulips on the nightstand. His exhausted eyes said, *Someday I'm going to paint this.*

In June, after the last round of treatment, I took him home. A week later, when he got the results of his bloodwork, he pulled me up from the table and waltzed me through the flat.

"I take it you're in remission," I said.

"For an American, you're pretty damn bright." He kissed me. "Yes, my love. We're safe."

"Right now, you mean."

"Right now, yeah."

"How long do you have to be in remission before you're cured?"

"Five years, Dr. Levitch said."

"Five yea—"

He put his hands on either side of my face and brushed his thumb over my lips, silencing me. "Shh, shh, don't trouble yourself with it," he said. "Think about today."

I smiled.

"There you go. That's better," he said. "Oh, God, I can't believe this. I want to get out of the city. I want to breathe wild air. Let's go to the seaside. Do you want to?"

"Well, if it's all right with Dr. Levitch, I guess—"

"Brilliant. Smashing. Okay. Curran," he yelled, "get your things together. We're going on holiday."

"This very minute?" came a call from the other room.

"This very minute."

"Bill, come on, don't be silly," I said. "I'm a mess, look at me, I haven't even had a shower, and the kitchen—"

"Forget the bleeding kitchen," he said. "We're free."

He turned and walked to the doorway, then ran back and kissed me again. "We're going to the seaside!" he yelped, and did a little leap into the air.

"You amuse me no end," I said. After he left, I slumped to the floor and laughed until I cried.

We drove to Dover and rented a guesthouse overlooking the beach. "You mean I get my own room?" Curran asked.

"Yes, you get your own room," I said, "but no beer and no loud parties, okay?"

"Okay," he said, giggling, and ran upstairs to check it out.

That night, while Bill got ready for bed, I stood on the balcony and watched the ferries make their way across the Channel, sending shards of light into the darkness. I wrapped my arms around myself.

"Honey," Bill called, "are you going to stay out there pretending you're Matthew Arnold all night?"

"No," I said, and came inside.

He sat on the edge of the bed in his boxers, shoulders hunched. For the first time, I realized how thin he'd grown. I ran a finger down his ribs. He shivered at the salt air. "I'm sorry," I said. "I forgot to close the door." I went back and shut it. When I returned, his teeth began to chatter. I untied the cardigan from around my waist and wrapped it around him. As I did so, my hair spilled over his bare scalp. I wanted to hold his ravaged body inside me so that, by some trick of the womb, I could let him grow again and begin over.

He drew me onto his knee. "I don't want to go back," he said. "Neither do I."

"I feel like London's ground zero, the epicenter of an earthquake," he said, "and if we just keep going, if we cross the water to France, and then further on into another country, pushing past borders, we'll get away from this thing. Remember when we went to Nice, right after we were married? Remember how great that was?"

I nodded, and thought of afternoons in an air-conditioned hotel on the Riviera. I'd wash the salt and sand from my hair, slip a pink sleeveless nightgown over my head, and crawl into bed beside him, droplets of water still clinging to my skin. Sunburnt, we'd doze, his head on my breasts, my palm on his back, until dinnertime, when I'd open the curtains.

"It would be so easy," he said, "to wake up Curran and take a ferry, to pretend our enemy were here and we could escape it, you know? But the enemy was inside me. And it could come back."

I stroked his collarbone. "This is a switch from the happiness dance you did earlier," I said.

"I'm scared."

"So am I."

Later, as he slept, I lay awake and listened to him breathe. I touched his face and he stirred a little. I put my palm to his chest, and it rose and fell. *Surely this counts,* I thought. *Surely this luminous moment matters.* And then I slid my knuckles down his side, down to the marrow, to where I knew that, despite the safety of numbers and reports, the terror would soon grow again, a thousand white cells coagulating deep in his hip.

• • •

The next morning I woke, reached across the sheet, and found it bare. Panic swelled inside my chest. I rushed out of bed and gazed around the room. Empty. I checked my son's room, the bathroom, downstairs. "Oh, Jesus, Bill," I said, and ran back up, heart pounding.

Then I saw that the door to the balcony was slightly ajar. I shoved it open and stepped outside. Ocean air whipped strands of my hair into my mouth, and I pushed them back. I shielded my eyes from the morning sun and stared down onto the beach.

Suddenly I glimpsed him. He stood with a towel around his shoulders in ankle-high water, barefoot, his trunks soaked. "Cold but terrific," he yelled.

I burst out laughing. It was one of those moments—tender, cinematic—which makes you feel as though you might shatter.

"You scared the shit out of me!" I yelled back. "Get up here."

Curran stumbled into my room and onto the balcony. "What's going on?" he asked.

I put my arm around him. "Your father's being a lunatic," I said.

He said, "Then he's definitely well now."

It rained that afternoon. I curled up on the sofa and read, while Bill and Curran went to Tesco's for groceries. They trooped back in with their bags, soaked.

"Look at you two," I said. "Drowned rats."

"I jumped in every puddle," Curran said, unpacking apples and cheese and a packet of Hob-Nobs.

"So I can tell by your shoes. And did you sneak in those chocolates?"

"No. Dad said I could get them."

"Well, okay, but no sugar highs, please, and put on some socks. That goes for you too, Bill."

Bill grinned. "Yes, Mum."

As they turned to go upstairs, I drew them both to me. "Things can only get better from here," I said.

Three glorious summer months. Of singing, of parks, of Bill's bruises faded. And then the bomb.

In September he relapsed. We tried to ignore the signs: blood in the sink every morning from his raw gums, pain in every bone, a host of new purple countries—Madagascar, Sri Lanka, Mozambique—which appeared on his arms. But we couldn't, and so on a day crackly with fall I took him back to St. Pancras for the same ten-day routine with the blue basin. This time, though, when I brought him home he was so drained that he leaned on my shoulder coming up the front walk, and the weather had turned colder, sharper.

Still he went to the studio. He'd arrive home smelling of turpentine and triumph, so worn he'd flop onto the couch and sleep through dinner. I'd sit on the floor and listen to him snore while I graded exams. Around nine he'd wake and lie there, silently play-

ing with my hair as I debated who got extra credit. "Sweetheart,"
I said, "you shouldn't work so hard."

"You don't understand," he said. "You know the saying about
running for your life? Well, I'm painting for mine."

I laughed. "I'm sorry. I don't mean to make fun of you, but
that just sounded like the name of a game show, the way you said
it."

"Yeah, it did, now that you mention it," he said, and put on a
deep-throated announcer's voice. "Now, live from the BBC, it's
. . . 'Paaainting for Your Life.' " And he laughed so hard he
scared me.

One November night he rolled against me in sleep, and I startled
awake. He threw his arm across my chest, in not an embrace but
in a desperate reflex. His limbs twitched. Sweat glittered in tiny
globules on his creased forehead. He licked his cracked lips and
let out a moist moan. He had a musky, iron smell, all agony and
perspiration. I held him still and pressed my wrist to his cheek.

With one hand I whipped the blankets back and thought: water. I propped him up, twined my arm around his waist, and led
him down the hall to the bathroom. When I flipped the light
switch, he lowered his head, rubbing his eyes, and cried out. He
leaned against the sink. His fingers fumbled with buttons as I
knelt on the linoleum to adjust the faucet. My knees ached. My
knuckles hurt. I tested the water, making it cold enough to stand.
I looked back and saw him slumped on the floor, back to the wall,
chin down at an uncomfortable angle, eyes closed, pajama top
half-open.

I guided him to his feet and held him there, easing the plaid flannel fabric off and down, sensing his shame at an intimacy born of dependence, not passion. I steadied him so his knees wouldn't buckle as he stepped over the rim of the tub. He kept his face turned away from me, gazing instead at the cracks in the wall tile.

There, on his back, he lay in the icy water. It made ripples over his yellow-black bruises. He tipped his head back, my fingers supporting it as if he were an infant, and for a moment smiled with sheer cool pleasure.

With a washrag I sponged the hollows of his neck and then swished the cotton through the water. Waves pulsed across his chest. His breath came in deep, ragged shudders. I sat and swished, sat and sponged. Slowly the shock hit his body. His shoulders quivered. He raised his hand, and with one thumb stroked the same place on my neck I'd bathed on him. The water dripped a wet splotch onto my nightshirt. "Thank you," he said.

Later, dressed again, he sat on the edge of the bed and I took his temperature. In the lamplight I strained to read the mercury. "Shit," I said. "A hundred and two. It's back up again."

He curled up on top of the quilt. "I'm going back to sleep," he said.

"No, you're not," I said. "Not until I call Dr. Levitch." We'd been warned that the drugs would make him susceptible to infections, which, though seemingly trivial, could be dangerous.

Dr. Levitch confirmed that this was one of them, so at three in the morning I helped Bill into his coat, shook my son awake and with a thousand apologies deposited him at Deepa Romdourl's, and drove Bill to the hospital. Between starched sheets he lay, parched and gleaming, as I sat beside him until dawn broke, and kissed his fevered wrist over and over, and made wild promises about Australia.

When he came home, he was so weak that at dinner his first night back, I had to hold the fork to his lips. He ate a few bites, then ducked his head against my shoulder and sobbed, "I'm sorry, I'm sorry." I patted his back. Curran stared at us, horrified. I motioned for him to leave the room.

Bill looked up. He made a noise deep in his throat. His mouth was so ulcerated that he had difficulty speaking more than a few words.

"Don't strain yourself." I tore the edge off one of my lesson plans. "Here. Write it down."

I put my hand over his to steady him. In a shaky scrawl he wrote in all capital letters: I DON'T WANT TO DIE, DAMN IT!

"Of course not," I said. "And you won't, sweetheart. This was just a setback. Dr. Levitch said it might—"

Before I could help him, he grabbed the pen again and wrote: YOU AREN'T GOD. YOU DON'T KNOW.

"No," I said. "I don't."

Those late-fall nights. We lay in bed, slightly shivery, loving the crispness. Moonlight turned him silver. I traced his mouth with my fingers and thought, Winter is coming, my angel, and we will have to gorge ourselves now before the famine.

.   .   .

He told me once how, during his fever, he'd seen me standing at the foot of his bed with my black hair swirling around my face and my head swathed in a nimbus of hues, vibrant reds and purples and blues, stained-glass church-window colors, like the woman in Russolo's *Perfume*. He'd screamed and screamed and tried to reach me, but couldn't.

"You had a temperature of a hundred and four degrees," I said. "You were hallucinating."

He wrapped his arms around me. "I don't care," he said. "I don't ever want you to be out of my grasp."

That night at dinner, Curran asked, "Do dead people remember?"

He went to the studio for the last time on a Saturday afternoon in mid-December. I drove over to pick him up. He came out in old jeans and a Navajo-print blanket coat, a red scarf tied around his bald head. "How'd it go?" I asked.

"Dead good."

From the backseat, Curran said, "Are you going to be famous, Dad?"

"I sure hope so," he said.

That was the day he finished *Necessary Madness*.

Christmas. The pipes froze. We made love beneath three quilts and drank coffee. His teeth chattered. The world was all holly berries and howling wind. He kissed my temple and said, "There will never be another moment quite like this."

The next day, Boxing Day, he woke feeling miserable. He had a slight fever, but neither of us worried about it. We figured he was just tired from the holiday rush. I gave him some aspirin and promised to keep Curran out of his hair, and, satisfied, he slept.

In the afternoon, though, he grew worse. He thrashed, sweating, breath raspy. I had to hold his head still to keep the thermometer under his tongue. I turned my back to him and read the mercury. My jaw dropped.

"It's . . . it's not as bad as last time, is it?" he asked.

Quickly I swung around to face him. "Oh, no, not at all," I said, "but just to be safe I think I should call Dr. Levitch."

I stood. He grabbed my hand and pulled me down beside him. "Stay here," he said.

"It'll only take a minute," I said, and kissed his forehead.

In the hall I passed Curran. "Do me a favor, love," I said, "and go sit with your father while I call the doctor."

"What's wrong?"

"He's got a bad fever."

"Will he be okay?"

"I think so, but he's worried. Go on."

I was about to call Dr. Levitch's home number when I heard a scream from the bedroom.

"Mum! Mum!"

I ran in and found Curran crouched on the floor in tears. On the bed, Bill's eyes rolled back in his head as his limbs jerked with convulsions.

"Get up," I said to my son. "I want you to get up and call an ambulance. Now."

He scrambled to his feet and down the hall while dumbly I just stood there, longing to touch Bill even though I knew I shouldn't, aching for a way to make him realize I was with him, a way to say, *Even in your most paralyzing pain, way down in your deepest darkness, my darling, I am there, I am there.*

Chapter Seventeen

The morning of the retrospective, I went into Curran's room and told him he couldn't go. He threw a pillow at me. "I hate you," he said.

"Go right ahead and hate me, then," I said, and closed the door behind me as I left.

My mother and I did the breakfast dishes to the sound of his sobs. "Don't you think you're being too harsh with him, Gloria?" she asked.

"No."

"But he's so interested in art, and he idolized his father so much—"

"I've made up my mind. He's not going."

"Why?"

"Because Bill's paintings are like autopsies. They detail thoughts and emotions that as an eight-year-old he shouldn't have to deal with."

"He's intelligent, though."

"And still a child." I handed her a plate to dry. "Besides, he's got to learn that the world can be cruel to intellectuals, doesn't he?"

She looked down. Blinked hard.

"You love to push the knife in deeper, don't you?" she said.

"No. I just want the truth."

I leaned up to put a glass back in the cupboard, and she touched my arm. "What?" I said.

"Trust me," she said. "You aren't another Riordan."

As night fell, I grew nervous. I picked at the roast beef sandwich on my supper plate and bit what little nails I had left. My mother sat across from me with a bowlful of water and her makeup bag, intent upon turning them into fabulous daggers. "Mom, come on," I said. "This isn't about me. This is about Bill. No one will notice."

"I know," she said, and smiled.

I didn't protest, understanding that this was one of her odd stabs at closeness.

"The first exhibit I went to that had Bill's work in it," I said, "was one right after Curran was born. Of course I was nervous and self-conscious about how I looked after that, plus I had this inflated idea of myself as the artist's wife, a dark, chthonic figure for all the photographers to snap pictures of, so I ended up sorely disappointed. There was no press in sight. It was dimly lit and smoky and trendy, and Bill seemed like the only person in the room with any shred of sincerity about his work. I felt like, Christ, why bother, what's the use of this charade? But now, this time . . . I don't know what I'll feel."

"Hold still. There's no way I can push your cuticles back while you're gesturing wildly."

"Sorry."

"What time do you leave?"

"Eight."

"Are you going by yourself?"

"No. Jascha Kremsky's taking me." I sighed. "Drop your eyebrow back down, Mom. It's nothing symbolic."

"But won't that look as if—"

"Yes, it might, but I don't care. I can't go alone."

"Yes. Of course not. You shouldn't." I winced as she filed the edge of my thumbnail. "Just out of curiosity, do you think he's interested in you?"

"He's not a lecher. He's gone through the same thing I have."

She looked up. "He has?"

"Yeah. Worse, actually. He lost his wife and daughter."

"Oh, God." She rifled through her assortment of bottles.

"Pick a subtle color, okay? I'm not exactly in the mood for 'fuck me' red tonight."

"Would you stop swearing like that?" Her tone admonished me, but then she grinned. "I left that shade at home, anyway."

After she finished her polish job, I went into my room, slipped on my stockings, and pulled out the cranberry Harvey Nichols dress. I'd just stepped into it when I heard a tentative knock at the door.

"Come in," I said, expecting it to be my mother asking if she could work on my hair next.

It was Curran, his head low with shame. He'd steered clear of me all day.

"Hey, kiddo," I said. "What's up?"

"I—I'm sorry," he said. "I really don't hate you."

"I know," I said, and touched his hair.

"Can I stay in here for a while?"

"Sure, if you promise not to throw any more pillows at me." I struggled with the zipper on the back of the dress. "Damn, it's stuck. Could you get this for me, Curran?"

He clambered onto the bed, swept my mother's robe aside, and on his knees pulled the zipper up the whole way. His small, soft hands rested briefly on my shoulders. "There you go, Mum," he said.

"Thanks, love."

I sat before the mirror and pinned up my hair. As I leaned forward to put on lipstick, I glanced sideways, waiting for some filament of Bill to materialize behind me on the bed and fiddle with his tie or advise me on which necklace I should wear.

But, no. There was only the pale orb of my son's face.

"Someday," he said, "could I see Dad's paintings?"

"When you're older."

"Are they good?"

"I'm no art critic," I said, "but they're honest, and that's all anyone can ask for."

"Gloria," my mother called from the kitchen. "Jascha's here."

I fumbled for my earrings, stepped into my heels, and gave Curran a kiss, then went out to meet him. "Your mum's incredible," he said as we walked down the front steps.

"Yeah, well, she acts like this is the fucking prom."

He laughed as he opened the passenger door of his car for me. "Sorry," he said, "but I forgot the corsage."

I went to nibble the corner of one polished nail as he got in beside me, but then balled my hand into a fist and stared out the window.

"You look nice, by the way," he said.

"Thanks."

"What's wrong?"

"Nothing, I—I just—I'm afraid of this."

We drove the rest of the way to Whitechapel in silence. "Oh, God," I said when we got there. "I didn't expect this many people."

"Don't worry," he said, and took my elbow as we went in.

At the entrance, there stood a rackful of pamphlets printed with somebody's analysis of each piece. I grabbed one and stuffed it in my purse, thinking I'd give it to my mother. Another little souvenir for David.

Inside, the crowds were thick. Less noise than I was used to permeated the gallery. There wasn't the usual off-the-subject chatter about the warmth of the wine, the difficulties of arranging publicity, or the latest independent film at the Everyman Cinema. People filed past the paintings with the studied silence of academics, glasses clutched in their hands, their black garb for once truly appropriate. I looked down at my dress and felt like a bloodstain, a siren wailing. Make way for the widow.

Bill's friend Jim came over and embraced me. "Gloria," he said. "I'm so glad you let us do this."

I smiled weakly.

"So how have you been?" he asked.

I made a wavering motion with my hand. "I'd be a liar," I said, "if I told you that I'm doing fine, but things are a bit better."

"That's good. You know what they say about time—"

"Healing all wounds, yes. But not without scar tissue, believe me."

I expected him to laugh, but then remembered that he wasn't Jascha. Behind my shoulder, a flashbulb went off. I jumped.

"Jesus," I said. "Are there photographers here?"

He nodded. "From the *Times*."

"I'm not one for self-flattery," I said, "but to be safe maybe I'd better get out of the line of fire. Good to see you, Jim."

I waved to him, and then wandered to the end of the line. Might as well look, I thought, and be anonymous for a while. I twisted my wedding ring and swallowed hard as I passed the

Lamberhurst painting. I tried to keep my gaze rapt but cool, and found I couldn't.

Jascha broke through the throng and came over to me. "Gloria," he said. I stood with my arms wrapped around myself, gazing at a portrait Bill had done of our son, and didn't hear him. He moved to touch my shoulder, but instead his fingers brushed my neck.

I startled. "Yeah?"

"We're about to start the—the, ah, presentation in a few minutes," he said. "I just wanted to let you know."

"Do I have enough time for a drink?"

"Sure. You need one?"

"Violently."

"Okay." He pointed to a table. "Right next to that woman in maroon."

I went over, took a glass, and stood against the wall. I had to admit that Jascha had done a good job. The backdrops were stark, simple, free of hype. White, the color of the cells which had gone wrong.

A young man joined me. He cleared his throat, sipped his drink, pushed his dark hair out of his eyes. A wiseass art student, no doubt—probably the Royal Academy.

We stared at the line of people snaking past the canvases, snaking towards the end of Bill.

"Isn't this amazing?" the young man asked. "Isn't it incredible how his paintings parallel his illness and resulting death?"

"There is no parallel to death," I said. For a moment I considered throwing my drink in his face.

He glanced over at me. "Did you know Bill Burgess well?"

"I was his wife."

Jascha waved from across the room. "Excuse me," I said, and walked over to him.

"Just a second, and we'll be ready," he said. "What's the matter? You look like you could murder someone."

"I had a little run-in with the intelligentsia."

"Fun, fun."

"Listen, there aren't going to be any newspaper types in hot pursuit of me, are there?"

"No, why?"

"I don't think I can answer deep questions."

"You won't have to." He led me over to a platform which had been set up with a podium. A murmur rustled through the crowd as it trickled towards us, and then there came a call for silence. Jascha climbed the steps and took his place. He adjusted the microphone, which gave the telltale squeak those things insist upon emitting in moments of high tension. *Please don't joke,* I thought. *Not now.*

"Good evening," he said. "We're here tonight for a bittersweet gathering, one of both celebration and mourning. Celebration, because there's joy inherent in the showcasing of an artist who deserves to be showcased, and mourning, since that artist could not be here with us to take pride in his work.

"I'm sure most of you are aware that Bill Burgess died of leukemia on January fifth of this year. You'll notice that I said 'died,' and not 'passed away,' or 'left this earthly sphere,' or any other euphemism commonly employed in order to mince around death. To use one would have been to deny what Bill's art was about: the truth, bare, controlled in its expression. In a time when pretension encroaches upon us, isn't it important to reward the unpretentious?

"And so we have done our best to honor Bill Burgess. Many have invested time and energy in this project, but those who deserve special thanks include all at the Whitechapel Gallery . . ."

As he spoke, I gazed at his black hair slicked firmly in place, at his flamboyant purple tie, at his eyes as they darted from us to the paper then back at us again. I imagined him as he must have been as a child—hyperactive, mischievous, smooth-talking, but painfully well-intentioned. I smiled.

". . . and also the members of the Chelsea Emerging Artists' Cooperative, particularly Sean Kennedy and Jim Welsh. Most important, I want to thank Gloria Burgess, Bill's widow and executor of his estate. Without her kind permission, this retrospective literally would not have been possible, and without her insight it would not have been as fitting a tribute to Bill. I've asked her to share with us a few thoughts on his work and his life. Gloria?"

Shaking, head down, I made my way up the steps, holding the folds of my skirt in my sweaty fingers so I wouldn't trip. Jascha nodded to me, and, before he left, squeezed my hand hard behind the podium. I stared out at all those intense, expectant faces, and tried to think of the tricks they'd told us to use so we'd relax while giving speeches back in high school Oral Communications. Look at the wall. Picture your audience in their underwear.

I tucked a strand of hair behind my ear.

"Hi," I said. "I've . . . I've got to admit that this whole concept gets me nervous, and I've got to warn you that what I'm about to say is neither a tear-stained eulogy nor an art history dissertation.

"What can I tell you about my late husband? Well, I could tell you that he patterned himself after Munch and, in his earlier, more conventional and less troubled years, Hockney, that he was kind to a fault, that he longed to go to Australia. I could give him to you in a slurred catalogue: artist-lover-husband-father-angel-protector-visionary-*dead*. I could get confessional and tell you how he was there for me, how in my darkest, most poisoned moments he was willing, so willing to pick up my wrist and suck the poison from the wound, to take the risk of holding the venom in his mouth those first few dangerous seconds.

"But that wouldn't suit the task at hand. My cries of 'I remember' wouldn't give you a true picture of Bill or his art, because memory distorts. It slips and spirals and gets lost in the private code of the one who remembers, her loose jargon of allusions, symbols.

"I think Bill realized the perils of this. He was not a man of gray. He saw the world in brightness and coherence. The universe was simple and gorgeous to him, and he wanted to capture it all, to pick it up and devour it easily as you would a piece of fruit—or flowers, if you're Robert Browning." A few people laughed. "This is not to say that Bill was blindly idealistic. He understood full well the chiaroscuro of living; he just chose not to dwell on it. Sometimes I wonder if his belief in the inherent goodness of things made it easier for awful ones to befall him.

"I'm not an artist by any means, but I do have a decent background in poetry, and when I think of the importance Bill's art held for him during his last few months, I'm reminded of a prose poem the Russian poet Anna Akhmatova placed in one of her books under the title 'Instead of a Foreword.' In it she tells of standing numbly in a prison line in Leningrad, and of a woman who whispers to her, 'Can you describe this?' Akhmatova replies that she can, and some semblance of a smile slips over the shell of the woman's face.

"Like Akhmatova, Bill equated his art with his survival. One time he told me, 'I am painting for my life.' In a physical sense, this statement is of course naive, impossible; all the canvases hung here tonight cannot resurrect him from the dead. But Bill knew that being a witness, that depicting the fear and doubt and terror of his struggle to live, was the only way to survive. Thank you."

I stepped down to applause. As I pushed through the crowd, I heard whispers. "So she's the woman in number thirty-six. . . ." "And wait, look here, he probably meant to portray her in number eighteen, too. . . ."

I ran to the rest room and splashed cold water on my face. My breath came in frenzied gasps. My eyes grew wet. I stared at myself in the mirror, glared, and thought, You are going to have to do better than this.

I sat on a folding chair by the sink and lit a cigarette. A girl came out of one of the stalls. Perky, short blond hair, challis-print dress. Probably another art student. Oh, neat. Let's go see the death paintings.

"Your mascara's running," she said.

"Oh. Thank you."

I rummaged through my purse for a tissue and watched her leave. God, is that woman ever unhinged, I heard her thinking.

Stop, I told myself as I wiped my eyes. You told your son he couldn't punch Nigel Clark just because he was mad at the unfairness of what happened, so don't be a hypocrite and go making monsters of everyone because of it. She was a nice girl. A kind girl. She wanted to keep you from embarrassing yourself.

I reached for another tissue and instead pulled out the retrospective pamphlet. I turned to #38, *Necessary Madness,* and skimmed its description. The words blurred. "Harsh, stark . . . symbolic of the parent-child . . . evokes questions of . . . perversity of grief . . . those who go on . . ."

Those who go on, I thought. Yes. We who have to live, to remember, to breathe after the loved one's last drawn breath. What about us? Where do we go when we go on?

We have several choices.

On one end of the spectrum, we can refuse to go on. We can pull a Riordan Merchant, whether it be with a knife, a bottle of pills, or a gun. Entranced by thoughts of reunion, driven by desperation, we can cop out. Fade to black. Bang. Crash. Game over. Enough people left hurting to rival the magnitude of our pain, the pain we swore no one could surpass.

Or, if we still want to watch the sun rise every morning, or are squeamish about plotting our own deaths, yet we feel on the verge of collapse, we can lean on others. Do it for decades. Become a sort of mournful moocher. Expect our children to blink back their tears and catch our salty rivers of them in their trembling cupped palms. Notch our scars into the skin of their unscarred bodies.

And what if we're afraid of inflicting pain? What if we're afraid to feel it ourselves? Then it's deep-freeze time. Automatic pilot. Psychic Novocain. Get up-brush our teeth-wash our hair-make breakfast-go to work-come home-eat supper-fall into bed. Don't think about it. Don't let the love or the anguish creep in. And then when it explodes, we are caught out in the open, no shelter, no mask, bones lit up, flesh torn.

There's got to be another option, I thought, *but what?*

"I don't know," I said aloud. I tossed the pamphlet in the trash, and then, cigarette in hand and regulation smile in place, went back out to the gallery.

The rest of the night was nebulous. I remember having three more drinks and telling a reporter to get out of my face, and then all of a sudden it was eleven-thirty, and everyone else was filing out into the night air, and Jascha and I stood alone in the empty brightness.

We stared at each other. I wanted to run from him, wanted to run through the maze of paintings to its end and find Bill waiting there, his arms open, his grin wide as he said, "Ha. Fooled ya, didn't I?"

Jascha took my arm. "We'd better go," he said. As he led me

out, I glanced over my shoulder at the canvases. So clean and neat, so boundaried.

"Are you happy now?" I asked when we got outside.

He looked up as he unlocked the car. "What in the hell is that supposed to mean?"

"You got what you wanted, didn't you?"

"Why are you being so bitter?"

"Answer my question, and I'll answer yours."

"Yes," he said. "If you mean that I put together a good retrospective and it went smoothly, yes, I got what I wanted."

"So are you happy now?"

"No."

I gulped. A tear slid down my cheek, and I batted it away.

"What's wrong?" he asked. "Was it the exhibit? Did I do anything out of line? Was there something in it we hadn't discussed that you didn't like?"

"No, no," I said, "not at all. For a minute there during your little speech, I thought you were going to tell some story about me, like, 'And then I wound up in the flat of this crazy bitch who came to the door in her bathrobe, and . . .' "

We laughed.

"I liked it, though," I said. "It was great. Very dignified. Very Bill."

He touched my wet face.

"So what's with this?" he said.

"Because—because he isn't—"

"Isn't here." He sighed. "Yes. Oh, God, yes."

He brought his hand down, and I grabbed it. He moved

closer. I brushed my lips across his. They were quick, starved empathy kisses—*I know, I know.* He reached his fingers up to the base of my skull, and yanked the combs from my hair. When we pulled apart, strands of it were in his mouth.

"Sorry," we both mumbled.

I leaned forward and wrapped my arms around him. "Owe me a beer," I said against his neck.

"What?"

"You owe me a beer. Didn't you know that's what you're supposed to say whenever you and someone else say the same thing at the same time?"

"No. I didn't."

"Well, you do now."

He stroked my back. "Honey, you don't need any more alcohol," he said.

"Yeah. Next thing you know, I'll be kissing a complete stranger."

"I lied," he whispered into my hair. "I'm not sorry."

"Neither am I. Mixed-up. Guilty. But not sorry."

We leaned against the car door, his arm around my waist, my head pressed to his shoulder.

"You know," he began, "I think Bill would have—"

"Shh," I said, and put a finger to his lips.

"That's right," he said. "I'm forgetting how, the last time I tried to tell you what Bill would have wanted, you slammed the door on me."

"Don't talk."

And so we stood there, silent in the darkness, holding each other, and as I watched the late-night traffic pass by and thought of my parents, I told myself, *We're not making their mistakes. We're not like them.*

He drove up to my building and we sat in the car for a while. I had a smoke.

"You really ought to quit that," he said.

"Yeah." I glanced past him and into the windows of my flat. All dark. "I'm surprised my mother's not inside with a stopwatch. 'Gloria, you've been out there with him for ten minutes! There's something going on between you two, I know it!' "

He laughed. "What, does she think there is?"

I nodded.

"Well, there is, isn't there?"

I tipped my head back. "You don't waste any time, do you?" I said. "I . . . I don't know what to call what just happened. There's no convenient Greek name to assign it. Maybe it was meaningful, or maybe it was a mere rush of hormones at an East End car park."

He reached for my free hand. I slipped it from his grasp and ran my fingers gently over the back of his neck. My nails shimmered next to his skin.

"Gloria," he said. He leaned towards me, lips parted. His eyes shone.

"No," I said. "Not now."

"Do you need me to walk you up?"

I shook my head.

"Can I call you?"

"I can't stop you," I said.

• • •

I went upstairs and stumbled into the kitchen, feeling my way through it so I wouldn't have to turn on a light and wake anyone. I banged my shin on the table, and clamped my hand over my mouth to muffle a scream of pain as I limped down the hall to my room.

Inside, I took off my heels and padded over to the closet, where I pulled out my pink French Riviera nightgown. It was an expensive one, and so had lasted all those years. By the light from the window I unzipped my dress and pulled off my stockings, ever aware of my mother asleep on the bed. I prayed she wouldn't see my bent figure, all glowing flesh, drunk, vulnerable. There was a bruise on my leg.

"Tanzania," I murmured.

"What?" came a moan from the direction of the pillows.

"Nothing," I said. My hands rose to my loose hair, and I fought to remember where I'd stuffed the combs after Jascha had pulled them out. I went back to the closet and found them shoved in my coat pocket. I threw them on top of the dresser. They stared up at me: gilded, innocent.

I thought of the slippery, ephemeral feel of Jascha's skin beneath my fingers, the salty, caustic taste of his mouth, the thick haze of his musky scent—all veneer, all polish, all fire, a foreign country, while Bill had been bland, visceral, smelling of oatmeal soap, earthen, like a homecoming. I took off my earrings and put them in my jewelry box. After a moment of hesitation, I left my wedding ring on.

I stealthed past my slumbering mother and down the hall. On my way to the bathroom, I passed my son's room. His door was ajar. I tiptoed past and stood by his bed. I stared at the pale, round half-moon of his cheek and listened to the steady, even rhythm of his breathing. He stirred. When he glimpsed me, he rocketed up, his hair rumpled.

"Mum," he said. "The exhibit. How was it? Were there famous artists there? Were there newspaper people?"

I smiled. "Here," I said. "Move over."

He wriggled to the other side of the mattress, and I crawled under the covers and put my arms around him. He rested his chin on my collarbone.

"You smell of smoke," he said.

"Yeah. Pretty awful, huh?"

"You should quit. If you don't, your lungs will turn to rubbish."

"I know. Jascha's been bugging me about that, too."

Speaking his name felt like both a benediction and a betrayal.

"So tell me about the exhibit," Curran said.

"It was nice," I said. "It fit your father."

"Will there be an article about it in the paper?"

"Probably. There were reporters there."

"Can I read what they wrote about Dad when it comes out?"

"Oh, if you insist." I kissed his forehead. "It'll mostly be journalistic babble, though."

"I won't mind if I can't understand some of the words. I'll just ask you. You're a walking dictionary, Mum."

I laughed. "What, not a thesaurus?"

"That too. Do you think Dad will be famous now?"

"That's not for me to decide."

"I think he will. Did you give a speech about him?"

I nodded.

"I wish I could've been there to hear it," he said.

"I know you do." I stroked back his damp hair. "You'd better get back to sleep, love. It's one in the morning."

"Really?"

"Really."

"Wow," he said.

I climbed out of bed and tucked the blankets back in around him. The image of us from *Necessary Madness* synapsed briefly through my brain, and I pushed it away. No, I thought. That will not be him. That will not be me.

After that I went into the bathroom and removed my eye makeup. I was about to blot off my lipstick when the nausea hit me. I leaned over the sink and turned on the tap to cover the sound of my throwing up four glasses of wine and my dinner.

My mother came in just as I wiped my mouth with a towel. I caught sight of her face in the mirror as she stepped behind me and put her hands on my shoulders. For a moment I expected her to yell at me—*It is one in the fucking morning, Gloria Merchant, and I really don't appreciate this*—but she didn't.

Instead she turned me around and gazed into my eyes.

"Gloria," she said.

I ducked my head and rested my cheek against the smooth, cool curve of her neck. "Mom," I said, "tell me that I'll make the right choices. Tell me that I'll be brave enough." Clad in floral silk, she smoothed back my tangled hair and stood barefoot on the linoleum tile and whispered, *You will, you will.*

Chapter Eighteen

London froze during Bill's last winter. I saw my breath each morning when, still in my nightgown, I crouched on the edge of our bed and dialed the hospital to hear if he'd survived the previous night. My lips moved in silent prayer as the wind howled, rattling casements.

Weary but polite voice on the other end of the line:

"Yes. He's stable."

Yes. A tiny snip of a word, but at that moment the most euphoria-inducing statement in the English language, the seven a.m. pivot upon which my life turned. *Yes* sent blood to the surface of my skin and pushed warmth into my icy fingers as I dressed in the gray dawn, pulling on layers of wool, wanting to open a window and lean out into the street and scream, "My husband is alive!"

Instead I'd go down the hall to wake Curran. He moaned when I slid my hand beneath the covers and shook his shoulder, but within seconds he always sat up and asked, "Is Dad all right? Can he come home?"

"Not yet," I said.

"Well, when?"

"I don't know. The drugs they're giving him take time to work."

"That's bollocks," he said as he climbed out of bed. "They should make him better"—he snapped his fingers—"like that."

"Don't swear," I said, but part of me agreed with him.

He complained each time I took him downstairs to Deepa's for the day. "Why do you get to see Dad, but I don't?" he asked, kicking at her welcome mat as we waited for her to let us in.

"Because there are rules that say you can't."

"Those rules are daft."

"I know, but be patient. You'll see him soon enough."

I didn't tell him about the one exception to the rule: He could come with me if his father was dying.

In Bill's hospital room we were encapsulated. The room was a white jungle, sticky with the heat which rose from him. Every morning at nine I stepped inside, closed the door, took off my coat and scarf and gloves, sat down on a hard-backed chair, and gave up all citizenship in the outside world. For hours I didn't move. Nightfall slanted across us, darkening the thin blanket that covered him, and not until then did I stand and reach above his bed to turn on the light, a glowing strip eerily similar to the spotlights in the galleries where his paintings once hung.

We didn't say much. When he and I spoke it was through raised eyebrows, brushing of thumbs, fingertips stroked in the hollows of palms, those necessary languages, those alternate tongues. He dozed, and I gripped his free hand, the one that wasn't numb from being stuck with needles, and waited for the mercury to drop. By spring, I thought, he'd be home. His hair would grow back. He could sleep in the sun on the balcony. We'd make real plans about Australia and drink mango tea, and only safe things would blossom.

When night crossed the border into morning, he gazed at me tenderly and rasped, "Go home. You must be exhausted." At that point, had he in that cracked voice told me to slice my flesh into ribbons, I would have gladly done it.

I stood again and bent to embrace him. His frail arms encircled my back. "Angel," he said. The word stabbed me, but still I went through the motions of strength, said all the calming murmurs: *yes, I'll be back tomorrow, yes, I'll send Curran your love.* Anguished scream caged, held inside for the goodbye kiss. Later, during the tube ride home, the wail tore its way through my body as I sat in the cold, gleaming darkness and licked my lips to taste the salt of his sweat on them.

• • •

Leaving him. The determined speedwalk down the corridor—
don't look back—and into the rotunda, past the nurses charting
every cell multiplied, every cell lost, in the dusky hush at their
stations. Into the elevator. Fists clenched tight. How many times
did I watch the grimy mirrored doors slide towards each other
and lift my hand to push the button which kept them from closing at the last instant? How many times did I choke down my
desire to careen through the halls, knocking over medicine carts,
leaving fallen interns in my wake, all to rush to his room and put
my ear to his chest, to whisper, "I'm here, I'm here," to make
sure his heart was still beating?

Before I left, as I stood in the parking lot, I always turned
around and peered up into the window I knew was his, comforted to see a white shard of brightness inside it. He slept with
the light on, like a frightened child, never wanting to be in darkness, ever. I strained to glimpse his profile, the outline of his bare
skull, whatever fragments I could. I hated to think of him alone,
at any uncomfortable angle. What could I do? What sign could I
give him? A wave would have been too cheerful, a blown kiss too
melodramatic. Powerless, limbs thick with fatigue, I picked my
way across the asphalt as the icy air assaulted my flushed face and
the wind blew all traces of his scent off me.

Each night I collected a drowsy Curran from the Romdourls',
leading him across a den carpet littered with Christmas toys, and

put him to bed, then sat at the kitchen table and went over the plans for my second term before I snatched four or five hours of sleep.

At three o'clock one morning, my son came out in wrinkled pajamas and asked, "Why is God so mean?"

On the thirtieth I decided to send Curran to stay with Bill's parents for a few days. I couldn't keep burdening Deepa, who had two children of her own to worry about. I explained to him that this way would be better for all concerned, but still I had to drag him to the car. "Better for who?" he screamed. "Better for you, you mean!"

He quieted as we drove to Lamberhurst. I didn't try to reason with him; the roads were so slick that if I spoke I feared I'd lose control. When I pulled in the driveway, he unbuckled his seatbelt and let it fly back with an angry snap. He rested his cheek against the cold windowpane.

"Is Dad going to die?" he asked.

"We're all going to die, Curran."

"Don't be stupid. You know what I mean."

"I can't tell you," I said. "The doctors say he isn't in great shape right now, but then again they said that last time—"

"So he might get better, or he might not."

"Yeah."

"I hate not knowing."

"I do too, love."

He scrawled his name backwards on the frosted glass.

"I want to be near him," he said. "And you. I don't want to be way out here where I have no idea what's going on."

"Curran," I said. "Look at me. I'm going to call you every day, and you'll know what's going on. Promise."

"You won't lie, or make things sound happy when they aren't?"

"Of course not. And if anything important happens, anything at all, I'll have Gran bring you back to the city."

"That second?"

"That second." I motioned him across the seat, and he slid over to me. He shivered. I drew the folds of my coat around him. We sat like that for a few minutes, his face against my neck.

As we went up the front walk, a light snow began to fall. I leaned my head back and caught a flake on my tongue. "Tastes like rum and Coke," I said.

He laughed. "That's disgusting, Mum."

He turned around and gazed at the fields and outbuildings which surrounded the house. His face was bright and red with cold. He looked so small holding his suitcase. "When I leave here," he said, "either Dad will be home or he'll be dead."

New Year's Eve. Bill's fever went down enough to put him in good spirits. He begged the nurses to sneak him beer. *He'll get through this,* I thought. *How sick can he be if he's pleading for some Guinness?*

"I talked to Curran today," I said.

"Yeah?"

"Yeah. He was all psyched because Gran was going to let him stay up till midnight."

He laughed. "I miss him."

With jittery, sweat-soaked fingers, he toyed with a few strands of my hair.

"Resolutions," he said.

"Sweetheart, last time I checked it was still this year. Aren't you being a bit premature?"

"No harm in that. Go ahead, tell me yours."

"Okay," I said. "Let's see. I resolve . . . to be as utterly perfect and goddess-like as I have been thus far in my life."

"Shut up."

"You asked for it. No, seriously, I resolve to stop taking advantage of people, not to yell at the fourth-formers no matter how pesky they get, and to quit cowering behind intellectual bric-a-brac."

"You're too hard on yourself."

"Yeah, well, it beats egoism. Your turn."

"I resolve to get out of this place," he said, "to get well, and to live with my arms flung wide."

He fell asleep soon after that. I woke him up at 11:55 and sat on the edge of his bed, and we turned on the television and rang in the new year. He leaned over and kissed me. "Everything is possible tonight," he said.

The next morning I got a call from the hospital. His fever had shot up to one hundred and six degrees. Any higher than that would be alchemy. Any higher than that would kill him.

• • •

Deep inside his smoldering haze, my husband slept, limbs suffused with fire. Outside, the sky turned blue-black. Streetlamps flickered on. People drew their coats in tighter and took the tube home. Rain sloshed in gutters, and still he burned.

Bill lay with his head turned towards me on the pillow. Lost weight had sharpened his features, given them angles, made him look harsh and hungry. Heat softened his flesh. He was all purpled wax-paper skin, both an infant and an old man. Taped to his wrist, inside a scarred vein, lay a needle attached to a thin line of tubing which dripped antibiotics into him.

I once read a story about Houdini and his wife, and how they planned his stunts together. Before he departed, he'd give his wife a goodbye kiss in front of the crowd, and she'd slip him a key to unlock his chains. I loved that image of her, pale, dourfaced in a wide-brimmed hat, the way all women seemed to look at the turn of the century, her cheeks flushed with anticipation as she leaned forward to feel the brush of his lips, the cold metal waiting on her tongue.

Night after night I sat beside Bill, feet close together on the gray-flecked linoleum floor, fingers twisted around a tissue in my lap, head tipped back. I longed to take his head in my hands and press my mouth to his, to give him the chance for freedom.

The third day of the new year, I walked into his room to find him thrashing. I rushed to the side of his bed and reached out a hand to touch him, but he shrank back. "Who are you?" he said. "I don't remember you. You aren't supposed to be here."

"Bill," I said, "it's me. Don't you—"

"Get out of here!"

In tears, I ran into the hall and begged someone to find me Dr. Levitch. "When he's in pain, he gets disoriented," he said, hands on my shoulders. "Go take a walk and calm down. We'll give him some medication, and in a few minutes he'll be fine."

I did as he suggested, and then returned to find Bill asleep, curled up, his back to me. He gleamed with sweat and innocence. After a few minutes, he woke and turned over.

"Hi," he said softly. "What's wrong? You look like you've been crying."

I told him what had happened.

"Oh, God," he said. "So this is how bloody awful it's become."

That night, shivering, I went up the front steps of my building in the darkness and thought, *I want this to be a movie.* I want to lean back in my red plush seat with a plastic carton of popcorn and watch this awful story unfold, and know I am no part of it. I want to weep at the scene of a woman in a black coat who walks into her empty flat to call her son in a farmhouse miles away, but I also want the reassurance of a sudden garble in the sound, a sudden splotch on the screen, to remind me that her agony is just on film. Most of all, I want to leave the theatre and find my husband waiting for me on the sidewalk, snow in his hair, mouth frosty against mine, arm snug around my waist as he asks, "So, how was it?" I want to walk out of this life like I'm walking out of a room. I want to be anyone but me.

. . .

January fourth. He woke in such pain that the day revolved around morphine. In the afternoon Dr. Levitch motioned me into the hall. "I don't think he'll pull out of this," he said.

There were no hysterics, no melodramatic exchanges. He just touched my arm gently, and I nodded. We gazed at each other, Levitch and I, like two conspirators whose plot had failed, two idealists whose hero had fallen.

After he left me I went to one of the banks of phones and dialed Bill's parents in Lamberhurst.

"Louise," I said, "you'd better bring Curran."

She drove to the hospital right away. I watched my son come out of the elevator, head down, hands stuffed in the pockets of his royal-blue winter jacket. He ran to me. I hugged him hard, then sat him down on a bench outside Bill's room, my arm still around him.

"Either it's good or it's bad," he said. "Tell me which."

"Well," I said, "your father is in a lot of pain, and his fever is very bad. Not many people with a fever as bad as his survive."

"But he could."

"He could, you're right, but the chances are slim."

"So Dad's probably going to die."

I nodded.

He toyed with the zipper on his jacket. "Can I see him?"

"That's why you're here, sweetie."

"Gran said that sometimes he's confused. She said I should be careful."

"There's no need to worry. Just don't say anything that might upset him."

"Will he know who I am?"

"Of course." I squeezed his shoulders. "Stay only a few minutes, though, okay? We don't want to tire him."

He stood and turned to me. "Aren't you coming along?"

"No. You deserve a bit of time alone with your father. Don't be scared. Go on."

He went inside Bill's room, and softly closed the door. Louise sat beside me. We stayed there in silence until Curran came back out, face tight, eyes wet. Louise and I both stood. I bent down and kissed his forehead. He slipped one hand into his grandmother's and one into mine, and then we went to the cafeteria for supper. Over tuna-fish sandwiches, our knees touching beneath the table, he leaned forward and looked into my face and said, "That was the last time I'll see Dad, wasn't it?"

After Curran and Louise left, I went back to Bill and sat beside him. Off and on we both slept.

At one in the morning he lifted his head, panicky, and called out. "Gloria."

"Yes."

"You aren't going to leave me, are you?"

"No. I'm going to stay right here, love."

"All night?"

"All night."

His features relaxed. He lay back on the pillow. There was no more of his usual talk about how I must be knackered, how I should get home. He smiled. "Good."

With one hand he patted the mattress. I got up from my chair and sat on the bed. Fumbling but instinctive, he brushed his fingers across the sheet until they met mine. I grabbed on tight. "Don't let go," he said.

For the next sixteen hours, I didn't move. I couldn't look at Bill's face. Instead I stared at a frayed thread on his pajama top, at its pearly buttons. I wanted to rip them open with both hands, put my head on his chest, and feel the muted throb of his heart inside his ribs, but I didn't. I might cry. I might hurt him.

At three o'clock in the afternoon he reached up, pulled me down until his lips were at my ear, shoved my hair out of my face, and whispered in a dry rasp. "What?" I whispered back. Though I couldn't hear him, I hated to make him repeat himself; at that point every word that came from his parched throat was a sacrifice.

"Please," he said. "Something for the pain."

He stared at me. I saw a sudden cramp in his gaze, like the tightening of a belt. His skin was liquid.

"Okay. Hold on." With my free hand I reached for the cord that hung above his bed, and punched the call button with my thumb. In a few moments, the door swung open. A white-clad figure stepped inside. Bill blinked at the light from the corridor. The nurse went to the side of the bed and injected the glistening painkiller fluid into the IV line. Bill moaned a little. She gazed over at me.

"Let me know if there's anything else I can do," she said softly. Her curly blond hair was pulled back so tightly I could see the vein at her temple throbbing. The tag pinned to her blouse said REBECCA. I remembered that that had been Pandora Brennan's original first name, and thought of my Leigh Street days, their angst so deliciously trivial.

The nurse left, and Bill sank back on the pillows. He coughed. It was a loose, scraping sound. He gagged a bit, tried to speak, but all that came out was a futile creak.

"Water," I said. With a tiny jerk of his chin he nodded.

I leaned over to the nightstand and picked up a full Styrofoam cup, careful not to press in too hard and risk its implosion.

With one hand I held it, and slid the other beneath his head to raise him. He fought, the lines in his forehead going deeper, saying, No, no, let me do it, fighting for those last small shards of autonomy. I put the edge of the cup to his lips. He drank in fragile, quick gasps. His whole skull bobbed with the effort. My hand jerked, and the water slopped down his throat, over his collarbone. He smiled. It was a crude, minuscule smile, but I almost cried to see his face gleam as it broke open with pleasure.

The cup's edges had gone moist and cracked. I leaned across, tossed it in the wastecan.

"You've got circles under your eyes," he said.

He reached for my hand, straightened it, lifted it to his mouth, and kissed my fingertips. Two hours later he was dead.

• • •

That night I took the tube home from the hospital and walked for a while on Upper Street. My hands cramped with coldness even though I stuffed them in the pockets of my coat, and my face stung. As I passed pubs and kitchen-gadget stores and wine bars, I thought, *Oh, God, there's no one here to hold me this time. It's happening again.*

I was crying by the time Deepa Romdourl let me into her flat. She smelled like flour and silk and homecoming, and draped a soft brown arm around me. I leaned against her shoulder and gasped long and hard, my tears of sheer exhaustion staining her peach sari.

She sat me down in the kitchen, patting my hair maternally before she turned to wash dishes. I rested my head on my arms and squeaked my thumb over the plastic tablecloth as I watched Curran, sprawled on his stomach on the den sofa. He'd stayed with her since school had resumed. It was almost ten o'clock. Bill had died at five.

Meanwhile Deepa's daughter, Vari, lounged on the floor beside my son, doing her algebra homework in front of the television. "Sodding polynomial," she muttered. Her mother frowned. Curran sat up, rubbed his eyes. I stood. Went over to him. Knelt down. He mumbled something drowsy about Dad, was his fever still bad? Leaned his head on my collarbone. His palms were hot at the back of my neck. I wondered if he could sense it, the palpable aura of morphine and last wishes that clung to me, but I didn't answer him. Instead I helped him to his feet and mouthed to Deepa, "You're a saint. Really."

I led Curran back to our flat, keeping him close to me as I flipped every light switch: the one to the living room, the hall, his bedroom, mine. I bit my lip as I guided him, all moans and yawns, into a pair of blue flannel pajamas. He slid under the covers, and I pulled them up to his chin and kissed him good night.

Then I closed his door behind me and tore out of my clothes and into an old shirt of Bill's, and then I crawled beneath a pair of freezing sheets, and somehow, I don't know how, I slept.

The morning after was a Sunday. That got me. The air was so soft and quiet with luxury that any moment I expected Bill to come in with unkempt hair and the Arts section of the *Observer*.

I heard the sound of feet padding to the bathroom and back. I waited until I heard a creak and the rustlings of bedclothes before I slid from beneath them.

Curran didn't open his eyes when I sat beside him. I shook him a little. He jerked. The sweetness, the anticipation in his gaze—more snow to cancel school tomorrow? Dad's gotten better?—cut into me.

I swallowed.

"Listen, love," I said. "Your . . ."

The kind euphemisms, the gentle lead-ins, reduced themselves to a rough gag in my throat. I'd forgotten to put on my robe, and shivered. I clutched his hand.

"Curran," I said. "Your father died last night."

With one convulsive snap he wrenched himself away from me, back turned, his cries dulled by the pillow he buried his face in, palm flung upward. Little-boy tears displaced themselves as tremors along his spine. I reached out to touch his shoulder and he flinched. Now I knew where the phrase "break the news" came from. Even the air that circled between us seemed fractured.

I got up and went into the kitchen and made a cup of coffee. I sat at the table and drank the amaretto and gave myself orders: inhale, exhale. I waited for the scream of aloneness to overtake me.

Chapter Nineteen

The morning after the retrospective, I woke on the couch, groggy and disheveled, to the sound of a ringing phone. My mother got it. I lay back and listened to her perky, polite voice as it drifted towards me from the kitchen. "I'm sorry, but she's asleep right now. . . . Yes, that was a long night, wasn't it? . . . Shall I have her call you? . . . Right, right, of course. Goodbye."

She came into the living room and sat on the floor beside me. Her face glistened in the sunlight. She wore a tiny gold heart around her neck. I'd never noticed it before. Probably a gift from David. I rubbed my eyes.

"Who was that?" I asked.

"Jascha."

"Oh, God."

"He wants you to call him."

I sat up and yawned. "I'm sure he does."

Her features tensed with concern. "Gloria, what happened?"

"I don't know," I said. "I mean, objectively I can tell you, but emotionally I—"

"You want to talk about it?"

"Not really."

I got up and went into the kitchen before she could ask another question, then poured myself a glass of orange juice and called Jascha.

"Hey," he said. "How are you?"

"I'm slowly regaining my mental faculties, thanks."

"I think we need to talk."

"Yes."

"Can I take you to lunch?"

"Today?"

"Today."

I watched my mother fold the sheets and blankets that had fallen off the couch.

"Gloria?" Jascha asked.

"Yeah?"

"Are you mad at me?"

"No. At myself, maybe. But not you."

"Listen, if you're tired, or you don't want to, I'll understand, but I really think we should—"

"Okay."

"Where do you want to go?"

"It doesn't matter. Pick somewhere."

"Can I trust that I'll find you suitable to been seen in public with by around, say, noon?"

"You can."

I went back into the living room. "Mom," I said, "would you have any great qualms about watching Curran for an hour or two this afternoon?"

She looked up. "No, why?"

"Jascha's taking me to lunch."

She opened her mouth to speak, then closed it again and returned to tidying.

"You don't have to fold all that," I said. "Really. I can take care of it."

She smiled. "I don't mind."

"Well, I'm going to run and take a shower, okay?"

I walked to the door and then turned. "Mom," I said.

"Yes?"

"I'm sorry if I've been treating you more like a baby-sitter than a houseguest."

"What are you talking about? He's my grandson. We have a lot of catching up to do."

"I know, but—" I swallowed. "I just wanted to say thanks. You've helped me out."

She pushed a lock of hair behind her ear, and for a moment I saw the girl in the wildflower-print skirt at Oxford. "You're welcome," she said.

After a shower, wrapped in my robe, I stopped by my son's room and stood in the doorway. Draped in pale-gold light, he lay with the blankets tucked around his chin, his face soft, his tiny, slender fingers outspread on the sheet. His breath made the sound you'd expect a flower to make as it opens. I wanted to run to him, and drop a thousand gentle wake-up kisses on his cheek, but I stayed still with my arms around myself.

Curran, I thought. Loving you, raising you, being both your parents now, is the acid test by which my strength is measured. Every time I hunger, every time my numb tongue crawls towards the feel of the open mouth of a stranger, every time my flailing arms and legs reach to wrap around the waist of a man who is not your father, I promise I will think of you. Of your hazel eyes filled with tears, of your silent face, cramped with anger.

That afternoon Jascha took me to a place overlooking Hampstead Heath. We sat on the terrace and ate simple pub grub, bread and cheese and Branston pickle. He had a copy of the *Sunday Times* with him, and he spread it out over the table and paged through the Culture section.

"The article's in here," he said.

"So soon?"

"Yeah."

I looked away as eagerly he read. "You're in the third paragraph," he said. "They called you 'shaky but statuesque.' "

"I hate New Journalism. Was it brutal?"

"Not too bad. 'Bill Burgess's works strive relentlessly for an expression of the archetypal, sometimes with clichéd overstatement, sometimes with astounding power.' "

"Stop. I don't want to hear any more."

He folded the paper. "Gloria," he said. "About last night."

I stared down at the table and shredded a paper napkin between my fingers. "God, that sounds funny," I said. "Like some line from a soap opera. As if it were some vague, incredible blur of passion. *Last night.*"

"But it wasn't funny."

"No."

He leaned back in his chair, rubbed his forehead.

"I feel like such a predator," he said. "Here you are, widowed only four months, and—"

"I'm not some trembling forest waif."

"I know you aren't. But it's just the idea that I would—"

"That I could—"

"Yeah."

"It was both of us. You know that. It wasn't like a sporting event, where we'd be able to run an instant replay, have it all measured, a matter of time or distance or whatever. 'Oh, yes, it was . . . him, making the first move with a lead of two thousandths of a second.' "

He laughed. "Has anyone ever told you that you're really fucking weird?"

I took a sip of water. "Everyone in the world except Bill, actually."

We paid for our lunches—or, rather, he did, despite my protests—and took a walk through the Heath.

"There's this part of me," I said, "that keeps asking, 'So what? You're in the same boat. You're both lonely. Go ahead. Go for it.' Then there's another part of me that wants to laugh last night away, pass it off as silly tipsiness.

"And of course there's the voice of the wedding ring, the voice of guilt that whispers, 'Oh, but poor Bill, poor darling Bill, you mustn't betray him.' There's nothing adulterine about what happened. Bill is *dead*. He's lying in a grave in a Lamberhurst cemetery. He can hardly object. So why does it feel like a betrayal?"

"The vows only go up to 'until death do us part,' " Jascha said softly. "They don't give us any rules for what we should do after that, do they?"

We sat down in the grass. On Parliament Hill, a thick-waisted father in an olive fatigue sweater stood behind his slender denim-clad son, hands over his hands as they guided a kite into the air.

"Since your wife died, have you ever had another relationship?" I asked Jascha.

He shook his head.

"Not in four years?"

"Four long years," he said. He reached up and ran his

fingers across my hairline. I grasped his hand and drew it away.

"You want an answer, don't you?" I said. "You want it to be straight and concrete and boundaried; either I'm in love with you, or I just want to be your friend, or I never want to see you again. But I can't give you an answer."

I gazed down and rubbed a worn spot on my jeans.

"You don't know how easy it would be," I said, "for me to fall in love with you. You're an artist, you're honest, you're empathetic, you've got a sense of humor . . ."

"You're not so shoddy yourself."

"But—"

"What?"

"I'm afraid. Of forgetting Bill—I mean, my God, it hasn't even been six months, and the sound of his voice—"

"Is slipping."

"Yes. Yes." I sighed. "That's the hardest part of all this. You understand."

"But is that reason enough for us to get together?"

"I don't know."

I checked my watch.

"Do you need to go home?" he asked.

"Yeah. I promised Caroline I'd be back by two-thirty."

We turned to each other.

"Listen," I said, "I can't—I can't make any big decisions right now. I don't want to hurt Curran, and I don't want to rush myself. So could we just—could we just live in limbo for a while?"

He leaned over and hugged me.

"Beats living in hell," he said.

When I came home, I found my mother and my son sitting on the living-room carpet, playing invisible instruments—violins, cellos, oboes—as they listened to Radio Three.

Curran put down an imaginary bassoon and said, "Did you have a nice lunch, Mum?"

I nodded.

"Did Jascha have a copy of the paper? The one with the article on Dad's paintings?"

"Yeah."

"Did you save it for me?"

"It's on the kitchen table."

He jumped up and ran to get it. I sat beside my mother. "You look like something's bothering you," she said.

I leaned back against the sofa. "Mom," I said, "when you first met David, was it hard?"

"Yes," she said. "Exhilarating, delightful—because he possessed a bluntness, a vigor, your father never had—but still hard."

"Did you feel guilty?"

"Yes . . . and no. You were right to yell at me the other day, Gloria. Because too many times I think I used the wretchedness of our marriage, the fact that your father was so unhappy—"

"More than unhappy. He blew his brains out."

"Okay, unstable, then. Neurotic. Suicidal. Whatever. But I used that fact as an excuse, a rationale, really. Because I felt freer than I ever had in my life after your father died."

"Did you . . . did you look for pieces of Dad in David? Did you try to make David into him?"

"No. No. In fact, I was deliberately attracted to David because he wasn't like Riordan. I knew too well the dangers of trying to make people over."

"The way Dad tried with us."

"Yeah. I never—I never again want to lead the kind of life I led with him," she said, "but when things between David and me get tense, or in certain moments, like when you and I were in Earl's Court that afternoon, I just . . . I just want to bring him back, to breathe good breath into him. I want him here in fragments: his excited hands, his voice that was like fingers stroking the pain away from a bruise. Sometimes I wonder if there was anything I could have done—should have done—that would have saved him."

"Come on, Mom. You were distant, sure. But he wouldn't have been satisfied. Not even if you'd thrown yourself at his feet. Because you were the wrong woman."

She looked away. Mozart poured into the room, and with her thumb she smoothed a wrinkle in her silk skirt.

"How much did you know about Adrienne?" I asked.

"When we were at Oxford together, he mentioned to me that his fiancée had died earlier that year. It worried me, the fact that his love for me had a desperate tinge attached to it, but—"

"You let your worry slide."

"I did. He was so vibrant, and intense. In hindsight I saw that that intensity was dangerous. I should have taken my nagging feelings more seriously, but when you're in love, do you psychoanalyze your lover?"

"Of course not."

"After you were born, he said you resembled her, and you did. The same dark hair. The same grave eyes. 'She is Adrienne reborn,' he wept. I got angry at him then. 'For Christ's sake, Riordan,' I said, 'she isn't her.' He wanted to name you Adrienne, but I refused. I didn't want you to carry those obligations on your shoulders."

I thought about that act of refusal she had performed. How could I thank her? Not the same way I had for the cranberry-colored dress and the dinner at Le Gavroche.

"But I did," I said. "Later."

She gazed at me.

"I know," she said.

"Did you know it then?"

She gestured at me helplessly. "I—I had an idea," she said. "I mean—after the whole deal with the name, the way he obsessed about how you looked like her, I had an inkling, and I was scared—scared that you might . . . that you might not be safe—"

"So why did you let him be a parasite?"

She dropped her head in her hands, massaging her temples as if the emotional strain of finding the answer had crossed into the physical realm and given her a headache.

"You don't want to answer the question, do you?" I asked.

She swung back up.

"No, but I have to," she said. "I let him because I was over-burdened and I wanted what he had. What you had, even."

"How do you mean?"

"You two were . . . singular. You had your passions. You were able to have them without guilt. Chemistry . . . lost loves . . . James Joyce . . . punk rock . . . whatever they were."

"And you didn't. Because you were trapped raising me and teaching."

"Not trapped. Culturally conditioned, definitely, and stuck sometimes. But I could've said no to all that in the first place, had I been stronger. That's the worst part, knowing I wimped out."

I heard Curran banging drawers in the kitchen.

"What are you doing?" I yelled.

"Looking for scissors."

"They're in the drawer to the left of the sink. What do you need them for?"

"I'm cutting out the article."

"Okay. Be careful."

"You have no idea how hard it is for me not to be a part of your life," my mother said.

"What are you talking about? You're here, aren't you?"

She sighed. "You know what I mean. Eight years. Eight years I write to you, and hope, and—"

"And what?"

"You don't write back."

"I did."

"A scrawled page every six months."

"I'm sorry my English degree failed you."

"Why are you being so bitter?"

"Why are you?"

"Because I love you. Because I want to be a part of your life."

"I understand that, but what you want can't happen overnight. It can't be all fun and laughter and togetherness."

"But—but that day—the day we went shopping . . . that was fun, wasn't it?" Tears glistened in her eyes. "Wasn't it?"

"Mom," I said. "Oh, Jesus, Mom, please don't cry. It was. It *was*. Don't cry. I'm being mean. I'm sorry."

A frantic, pacifying tone crept into my voice, and, remembering my father, I grew silent. She recognized my panic, and put a hand on my arm.

"No, Gloria," she said. "I'm the one who should be sorry."

"Stop. I hate these apologizing marathons. We're both sorry. Let's get over it."

She laughed. "Good call."

"Bill always liked you," I said. " 'Come on, love,' he'd say. 'She's your mother. You ought to keep in touch with her.' Okay, I said, I'll send her a little postcard like the ones from the gynecologist's they send as a reminder when it's time for an appointment, to remind her that I still care. He didn't think that was very funny."

She grinned.

"I understand what you said," she said, "about things not happening overnight. Maybe I do expect too much too soon. You will write to me and keep in touch after I leave, though, won't you?"

I nodded.

"I really think being together here has drawn us closer, don't you think?"

"Yes," I said.

After that I went back into my room and slept. I needed time to lie on my back, on my own bed, and fall into oblivion, to digest my feelings towards Jascha and Caroline inside a cocoon of blackness.

When I woke again, the flat was draped in the softness of early evening. I got up and followed the sounds of my mother and son's voices to the kitchen. I leaned against the door with my arms folded, watching them.

My mother stood at the stove, where Bill used to stand, wearing the green apron Bill used to wear, the sleeves of her pink blouse rolled up. The soup she ladled into bowls was steamy and hot. I gazed at her hands steadying each bowl, holding its rim, and a part of me cried out, blood rushed into my fingers. I wanted to lean against her. I wanted to thank her. For vegetable soup. For trying. She looked over, smiled. Her face was thin, every bone pronounced, girlish. "You're up just in time," she said.

The three of us took our bowls to the small Formica table and sat down. Our knees softly touched. The steam warmed our faces. We ate in silence, crossing a border together into a room where the end was only the beginning.